PRAISE FOR *BLUE NOTES*

"Part suspense novel, part character study, *Blue Notes* takes us into the world of Big Pharma, greed, and the pathologization of emotion. But at its heart, it is a touching meditation on love and loss and what it means to be truly human."
—Elyse Friedman, author of *The Opportunist*

"Like watching a beautiful wound heal over, *Blue Notes* embraces the necessary scars that hold us together."
—Andrew F. Sullivan, author of *The Marigold*

"A captivating novel about grief, science, and love.
I was hooked from the start."
—Anettes Litteratursalon

"This formidable thriller is endowed with undeniably literary traits: rich characters, multiple storylines, and an unexpected twist…an explosive finale."
—*L'actualité*

"A gripping story, effective, and deliciously confronting… Brilliant."
—*Chatelaine*

"*Blue Notes* is a well-written, well-oiled novel of contemporary relevance."
—*Jyllands-Posten*

"An exciting novel, a real page-turner!"
—Librairie le Tumulte

PRAISE FOR AGATHA

"*Agatha* is a seductive tale, pleasingly spare and evocative…
Told with tenderness and humour."
—Martha Baillie, author of *There Is No Blue*

"With deft sagacity, Anne Cathrine Bomann reveals how the
possibility for transformation lies coiled within any life."
—Catherine Bush, author of *Blaze Island*

"This might be the universal read we all need."
—*Toronto Star*

"An utter delight…by turns poignant, funny, and sad."
—*Zoomer Magazine*

"Astounding."
—*Frankfurter Allgemeine Zeitung*

"A shrewd, skillful tale of loneliness, the search for meaning and a
place in the world, and the problems of truly relating to another
human being."
—*The Independent*

"Charming, funny, and packed with insight."
—*Irish Times*

"A quietly uplifting masterpiece."
—*Stylist*

Blue Notes

ANNE CATHRINE BOMANN

Translated by Caroline Waight

LITERATURE IN TRANSLATION SERIES

Book*hug Press | Toronto 2024

This translation was made possible through the generous support of the Danish Arts
Foundation.

**Danish Arts
Foundation**

Library and Archives Canada Cataloguing in Publication

Title: Blue notes / Anne Cathrine Bomann.
Other titles: Blå toner. English
Names: Bomann, Anne Cathrine, 1983- author. | Waight, Caroline, translator.
Series: Literature in translation series.
Description: Series statement: Literature in translation series | Translation of:
     Blå toner. | Translated by Caroline Waight.
Identifiers: Canadiana (print) 20230481914 | Canadiana (ebook) 20230481949
     ISBN 9781771668675 (softcover)
     ISBN 9781771668712 (EPUB)
     ISBN 9781771668699 (PDF)
Classification: LCC PT8177.12.O43 B5313 2024 | DDC 839.813/8—dc23

Book*hug Press acknowledges that the land on which we operate is the traditional
territory of many nations, including the Mississaugas of the Credit, the Anishnabeg,
the Chippewa, the Haudenosaunee, and the Wendat peoples. We recognize the
enduring presence of many diverse First Nations, Inuit, and Métis peoples, and are
grateful for the opportunity to meet, work, and learn on this territory.

For Rita
Who reminded us that love truly is the greatest of these

April 2011

———

ELISABETH

ELISABETH LOOKED INTO THE NURSE'S eyes and tried to understand what she'd just said. Grey eyes, with streaks of something darker, and if she stared long enough it was as though they lost all meaning. They became something someone had spilled, two murky stains that might at any moment dart elsewhere on her face.

"Autopsy?" she repeated.

"I realize this is a difficult thing to wrap your head around, but if we can find out what went wrong here, Winter might be able to help prevent the same thing happening to another little boy or girl." The nurse put her hand on Elisabeth's arm. "Actually, for some parents, it can make an unfortunate situation like this a little less meaningless."

At last Elisabeth blinked, taking a step backwards to escape the clasping hand. "I'd rather you didn't touch me, if you don't mind," she said. "And stop talking about cutting into my son. He's right over there, and he isn't dead yet."

The nurse pursed her lips, deepening the smokers' lines around her mouth, and it struck Elisabeth how incredibly ugly she was in her shapeless scrubs. The dirty hair and grown-out roots.

"Thank you," she said, turning her back. "I'd like to be alone with him now."

She went over to the bed. Winter wasn't there anymore, that was obvious. Only the body under the oversize duvet, curled gently in all that whiteness, surrounded by machines like lapping mechanical waves. She realized she'd started breathing in time with them again.

"My little heart," she whispered. "I don't want to be here without you."

And she didn't. When she imagined leaving Winter here, when she thought of getting into her car and driving away while he stayed, there was such a fierce shudder in her chest that for a moment she thought she'd lose her footing.

So there she stood, trying not to think of anything much. Just letting the seconds run over her like water. She stroked Winter's downy cheeks, grinning at the sight of his little milk teeth pressed into his lips, almost as though he were sitting on the floor back home, engrossed in one of his drawings. His hand did not respond when she squeezed it in hers, but she squeezed it anyway.

Mom. His voice struck her as soon as she closed her eyes. *Come and look, I've drawn a spaceship!* Her little boy, conjured by years of injections and hormone treatments, perfect on the surface, but with the sickness lurking underneath his breastbone. Would it have been easier to lose him if it had happened in one swift tug? In a car accident, maybe, or after a bad fall at the playground? She had no idea. She knew only that this was the worst thing that had ever happened to her, the most impossible.

"I'm going now, my little darling."

She whispered very close to his ear, telling him there was nothing to be scared of. She kissed him and stroked his hair one last time. Then she straightened up, her head swimming from months of fear and lack of sleep.

In the corridor outside, she bumped into the nurse from before. "You can switch them off now," she said. "But you're not cutting him open."

The nurse looked like she was about to say something, but Elisabeth continued past her, making for the exit. The hard clack of her heels was flung up against the walls and back into her face like a slap. "But aren't you going to be there, then?" the nurse called after her. "Elisabeth, aren't you going to come and say goodbye?"

CHAPTER ONE

September 2024

———

SHADI

IT WAS EMIL WHO SUGGESTED Shadi go somewhere other than home to write.

"Don't you think it would be a good idea to get out a little bit?" he asked, and she had thought it would be hard to concentrate. But it turns out the panoptic effect of other people's glances and their diligently hunched backs keeps her going. And not just that. All the rituals that run like paths through familiar terrain back at the flat—they've got no room here, where everything is new.

She opens her dissertation. The first task must be to try to distinguish between normal grief and the kind that was given its own diagnosis a few years back. Persistent grief disorder. When she looks it up in the International Classification of Diseases manual, she finds various symptoms that must be present in order to be diagnosed. For one thing, the event the person is grieving must be at least six months in the past, and it also must be a bereavement. It's not enough, as she first thought, to simply get divorced or lose your job or something, no matter how bad that might feel.

The reading room smells of warm, summer-browned bodies and bags containing packed lunches, which people take to the public areas in the library or the park across the road. Some people write with music in their ears; others sag over the tables and doze until they wake with a start, peering guiltily around them. A guy with a beanie is snoring gently to her right. Someone has opened a window, and the wind plays with the rough curtains. Glancing at the clock, Shadi decides to finish the section she's working on, although her belly is crying out for food. Forty-five minutes later she grabs the box of yesterday's leftovers and walks out alone into the sharp light, while her cardigan saves her seat.

Returning from her break, she goes first into the kitchenette, where another guy from the reading room is pouring water into two stacked plastic cups. He turns toward her and smiles, so she feels obliged to stay.

"You want one?" he asks.

"Yes, please." She follows him with her eyes as he pours in far too much water and puts the kettle back on to boil.

"Guess you're writing a dissertation too, huh?"

She nods. "Psychology. What about you?"

"Political science." He rolls his eyes. "Puts you in dire need of some instant coffee after lunch, doesn't it?"

He opens the fridge, takes out the plastic bottle Shadi herself put in there that morning, and pours milk into his coffee. *Hey*, she wants to say. *Hey, don't do that.* But she says nothing, just stands there feeling the glint behind her eyes as he turns the bottle upside down and shakes out the last few drops.

"Right, back to the grindstone." He gives her a wink, but her face is stiff and uncooperative. On his way out of the little kitchen, he steps on the pedal of the garbage and dumps the bottle, chosen specially at Netto and rinsed late last night with scalding water as she stood at the sink.

"Have fun!"

After that, work slows to a crawl. She keeps replaying the scene from the kitchenette, imagining all the things she should have said. *Hey, you do know that's my milk, yeah?* Anyone else would have spoken up, wouldn't they? Or they would have offered him a bit, just so long as there was still some left, and then everything would have been fine. Why is that always so hard for her?

Bit by bit, she gets back into her rhythm. She hauls piles of articles about grief out of her bag, leaning forward to decipher the fine tracks of the lettering across the paper, taking meticulous notes on everything she can use. As the hours pass, the reading room empties around her, and by the time she finally decides to head home there are only two of them left. Shadi and a thin, red-haired girl in the corner, who apparently lives off the jumbo raisins in the jar in front of her.

Shutting her laptop, she stretches her aching back. The song she's had in her head for days comes back as soon as she gives her thoughts free rein. How does it go again? They sing it at family parties—on the rare occasions they're all together—and although to Shadi's great regret her mother never taught her or her little sister Persian, the rhythm is alive inside her somewhere.

Against the background of the tune, she walks home through the city. The sun hangs large and heavy on the horizon. Today, for once, she's the one coming home late. Emil is on the sofa with his computer in his lap when she walks through the door, and he looks up. She goes over to him, still wearing her jacket. There's a certain power in being the one awaited, she thinks as she kisses him. The one who comes in from outside and sets the air in motion.

THORSTEN

LOOKING UP EVERY SO OFTEN from his notes, Thorsten registers the September sun like a warm hand against his cheek. On the university lawns outside the window, kids are sitting in groups on the grass, and once in a while their shouts reach him even in the office. It would be a nice change to sit outside and have a chat with them, but there's rarely time for that these days, and anyway, he's expecting a visit.

When he reads the keywords he jotted down after his first meeting with Birgit, it's easy for him to recall what she looked like. Not her clothes or her hair—he's not so into that type of thing—but her stooping posture, which added several years to her actual age, and the way she kept folding her damp tissue over and over. Seems like not much has changed, he thinks, when he pokes his head out and catches sight of her on the bench. Her hands are shaking weakly; all her movements are hesitant, as though protracted in time. Once she's finally gathered up her things, he leads her over to the sofa.

"So here we are again," he says, smiling, but Birgit's only response is a vague grimace. "Can I offer you something? Maybe one of these?"

He holds out the biscuit tin. "Today is the last time we're going to meet. So for once there are no questionnaires to fill out. We're just going to have a little chat, and I'm sure we'll wrap the whole thing up nicely."

She nods. The vanilla biscuit is a foreign body in her hand. She sits crumpled on the sofa, and Thorsten can't help comparing her with his own mother, who is around the same age but radiates an entirely different aura of vitality.

"I'd like to tell you again how happy we are that you wanted to be part of our project," he says. "It will make a tremendous difference for a lot of people. We're busy analyzing the tests you and the other participants have completed, and it won't be long before we get a general grasp of things."

"And then you'll figure out if the pills work?"

Birgit's eyes are red along the lower lid, as though they're turning wrong-side out. She looks ill, thinks Thorsten, but then again, she's looked ill for as long as he's known her.

"Yes," he says, "and how, crucially. We're especially interested in what occurs in the brain when people take the pills, and how they affect the way you grieve."

Suddenly Birgit seems to become aware of the biscuit in her hand. She takes a bite, her jaws driven as though by an invisible motor that might lurch to a halt at any time, and she looks exhausted. Thorsten wants to do something for her but doesn't know what, so for lack of a better idea he pours water into her glass.

"Once everything is ready we'll be in touch, and you can read our conclusions for yourself. Of course, neither of us knows whether you've had the placebo or the active treatment, but—"

Birgit cuts him off. Instantly her eyes are watchful, fixed on his. "If I've been getting the real pills, then that garbage doesn't work, I can tell you that for sure!"

Thorsten nods. "You're still very upset about your husband's death?"

She brushes a crumb off her trembling lower lip. "It's the same as it's always been."

Thorsten leans forward in his chair. They're so different, these final conversations. Just this week he's spoken to a young man who kept repeating how grateful he was for having taken part, but obviously there have been a few disappointed participants too, people for whom this is another hope lost. That's just the nature of the beast.

"I am sorry about that," he says. "I think you should talk to Miguel about it. He'll be letting you know if you've been getting Callocain or not." He raises his hand to signal that he's understood Birgit's opinion on that topic. "And he's also the one who will look after you going forward. You will get the help you need, Birgit. I promise."

Once she's gone, Thorsten opens the window. He has a few minutes before his session with Mikkel, the last patient before his part in the trial is definitively over. All the tests have been carried out, he has spoken personally with nearly two hundred of the four hundred or so participants, and although there have been a few stumbling blocks along the way—as there always are in clinical research—they've exceeded all their expectations. Not only is this the first study of its kind to focus on grief, but it also has the quality he prizes most highly in his working life: it's going to make a difference. It's not going too far out on a limb to say so, surely, because no matter the results, they will affect the way people with persistent grief disorder are treated and understood in the future. This study will help to define the approach to grief in Denmark, and if that's not worth showing up to work for, then he doesn't know what is.

He checks again but the corridor is empty, and after another couple of minutes he looks up Mikkel's number in the list of participants. The phone goes straight to voice mail.

"Hi, Mikkel, Thorsten Gjeldsted from Aarhus University here. I'm calling because we had an appointment at one-thirty, and you haven't turned up. I'll be in the office for another couple of hours yet, so if you can make it when you get this, you're welcome to drop by. If not, I'll try to catch you in the next day or two. Bye!"

Mikkel's story is the one that has made the biggest impression on Thorsten. He and his little family were involved in a car accident at a junction on Silkeborgvej, and in the days that followed, first his girlfriend, then the couple's newborn daughter, died of their injuries. Describing her brother at an introductory session, Mikkel's sister Louise had painted a picture of a well-liked and socially active young man who was perhaps a little too much of a live wire. Mikkel, just like Louise herself, had emerged surprisingly unscathed from a pretty troubled childhood. But ever since the accident he'd been doing steadily worse. Eventually, all his sick days lost him his job as a teaching assistant, and by the time the trial started, he was literally struggling to get out of bed.

A gust of wind knocks some papers to the floor, and Thorsten shuts the window. It's his distinct impression that Mikkel has been doing better over the past couple of months, but he's still keen to wrap things up properly. There's an increased risk of suicide when people are grieving, and although thankfully they've had no deaths so far, it's always the first place his mind goes when someone misses an appointment. The last thing he does before he leaves the office that afternoon is to call Mikkel again. But still, there is no answer.

ANNA

SOMETHING IS TICKLING ANNA'S NECK. Without opening her eyes, she burrows deeper into the warm nest of the duvet, but then there it is again. An insistent tickle, this time on the part of her shoulder that's exposed. She flaps her arm irritably.

"Good morning!"

She blinks a couple of times to get the sleep out of her eyes. The unpleasantness that results from too many drinks and way too little sleep washes over her like momentary seasickness.

"Hitting you pretty hard, eh?"

He smiles. He's pretty cute, actually, with those dark corkscrew curls. She has no clue what his name is.

"How are you so awake?" she yawns, wondering if she's up to having sex again before he takes off.

He props himself up on his elbow and gives her a kiss. "You talked in your sleep last night," he says. "Something about your mom. Do you remember what you were dreaming about?"

Anna shakes her head. The night has been reduced to black, just the way she likes it. But she's uneasy about a stranger hearing her talk in her sleep, maybe even leering at her as she spoke. Your face betrays you when you're sleeping, she knows that.

On her way to the bathroom, she's annoyed with herself for always sleeping naked. She's got to start keeping some underwear lying around for when she brings someone home.

"You want to grab some food?" he calls after her.

"Sorry, I need to be at the university in half an hour, so…" She shuts the door behind her and sits down on the toilet.

"What about a shower together?" she hears him shout. "Or a couple of kids, at least? Terraced house in Vejle?"

After she's splashed cold water over her head, she wraps a towel around herself and goes back out. He's standing in the corridor, putting on his shoes.

"Where do you live?" she asks, and he tosses his curls.

"Down by Tousparken."

He edges past her and grabs his jacket, avoiding her gaze. She feels sorry for him despite herself.

"Why don't you take an apple or something?" She trudges into the kitchen and stares down into the empty fruit bowl.

"No thanks."

"No." She goes back into the hall. "Look, I'm the weird one here. I just don't like playing this whole game afterwards. It's got nothing to do with you."

They pause for a moment, staring at each other, then he reaches for the doorknob. "Thanks for last night anyway, it was nice. Take care."

She smiles at him. After all, it's not his fault she talks in her sleep.

"And say hi to your mum!"

The words hang vibrating in the stairwell until the outside door slams behind him, shattering the echo into pieces.

Half an hour later she's ready. It's the first time in weeks that she's been out in the morning in anything but Everlast sweatpants. The bike creaks beneath her. First gear is useless, but she struggles half-standing up the hill until she can turn down Vestre Ringgade near the Old Town. The first drops of sweat are trickling between her breasts just as she parks outside the Psychological Institute.

"Knock knock."

Thorsten is sitting at his overburdened desk, apparently engrossed in the scraps of paper in front of him.

"Anna!" he exclaims when he looks up. "What a surprise!"

"I was just passing, and I thought we could talk about my dissertation if you've got a minute."

Thorsten takes off his glasses and sets them down in an empty spot on the windowsill. "Looks like someone was out getting hammered last night," he says. "Why don't I start by getting us a cup of coffee?"

While he's gone, she plops down into the worn armchair and glances around. If possible, it's even messier in here than the last time she came around, sometime before the summer break. There are stacks of academic books and compendiums on every conceivable surface, and the stuffy odour of printing ink reminds her, as always, of the library at her old school.

"I've been thinking of writing about the diagnosis of grief," she says, once he's returned. "Critically, of course."

He puts two cups on the low coffee table, moves some files, and sinks into the chair opposite. The aroma of coffee makes her empty belly growl.

"Grief?" He narrows his eyes. "Is that really such a good idea?"

"Why wouldn't it be?" she asks, but continues without giving him time to answer. "So, you on board?"

To her astonishment he shakes his head.

"I'm sorry, my friend, you're too late. I've filled all my supervision hours already. It's pretty straightforward, actually, what with this whole top-down approach. I'm not allowed to take on any more, no matter how much I want to."

"Are you serious?" Anna had never even considered this possibility. She'd seen asking Thorsten almost as a formality. "Maybe I can see if Svend likes it," she suggests without really meaning it.

"You can try," Thorsten says, "but I think he's in more or less the same boat as I am. Neither of us has a lot of time this semester because of the grief project. You're too late."

"Thanks, you mentioned that already." She leans forward, resting her pounding head in her hands for a few seconds before straightening back up. "This is bullshit." Clearly nothing's going to go right for her. "And my application's just been rejected by the faculty committee too. I've got to retake neuro." She keeps her gaze fixed on the floor so that Thorsten doesn't see the water level rising in her eyes. She sniffles hard. "It's so fucking annoying."

The springs in the armchair give a squeal, and a moment later Thorsten is standing beside her with a red napkin adorned with some dumb Christmas scene. She blows her nose in the middle of the angel's wings.

"You'll see, it'll all work out," he says, patting her arm.

She pulls a face. Right now it definitely doesn't feel like that. She'd really thought they would let her pass. She'd handed in all the assignments she was supposed to—the only problem was that she'd had too many absences.

"Let's put our thinking caps on, all right?" continues Thorsten. "Maybe you could join forces with one of the others, what's her name again…" He starts rummaging through the piles of paper on his desk and eventually draws out a notepad, turning it toward the window so he can read it. "Shadi. She's writing about grief too, and who knows, maybe you'll hit it off. It only means an extra one or two supervision hours for me. I'm sure I can sneak that into the spreadsheet."

Anna rolls her eyes. She knows Shadi from a couple of classes they've had together. She remembers her best from stats, where Shadi was almost eerily sharp in a very understated way. She's the type of person who lives to problem-solve, but Anna still hasn't heard her formulate a single independent opinion on the subject she'll soon have been studying for five years.

"You know what, I think I'd rather try my luck with Svend."

"You could also consider changing your topic," says Thorsten. "Not to interfere, but—"

"Well don't, then!" She cuts him off. "I'll figure something out." She lobs the crumpled napkin at Thorsten's garbage can, hitting the top of the inside hard and only just getting it in. She grabs the cup, ready to down it. This conversation isn't going at all the way she'd thought.

"I think she's writing in the old national library, if you want to try to catch her."

"Ouch, Jesus!" Anna slams the cup back down irritably, coffee burning all the way down her throat. "What did you say? Who's at the library?"

April 2011

———

ELISABETH

In those first days Elisabeth was silent. There were no thoughts, no tears, and when her senses again began to function and she found herself in Winter's bed with her face in his duvet and her nose buried in his scent, it hurt so much she wished she had never woken up.

She'd been afraid of losing him since the day he was born. He came out much too soon, quiet and blue, and those blue notes had settled across their lives like a special cast of light. The first operation took place immediately after the birth, and afterwards it was a long time before she was allowed to bring him home. Still, she was eventually allowed to lay his little body with its transparent fingernails and fluttering pulse against her chest. She had breathed warmth into him, praying that his heart would be strong enough to beat on its own, but it wasn't until the day she waved goodbye to all the familiar faces on the ward and staggered out to her car with her son in her arms that she truly let herself believe in his existence. She called him Winter, even though he'd been born in the spring, because he was so pale, and she had to rub his toes and tiny fingers to get the blood circulating.

Nala lay apathetically at the foot of the bed. It was impossible to know whether the dog understood anything or whether it was merely reflecting her own stagnation. Elisabeth only let her out into the garden these days. She could barely carry out the rudimentary movements required to give the dog food or change the dusty mirror in its water bowl. Everything hurt. It felt like she had the flu: grief is like arthritis, she thought, grief is a sickness that devours you. The phone rang, but she didn't pick up. She just lay there on the bed, occasionally stroking Nala's head, meeting the dog's brown eyes and closing hers again.

Weeks passed. She got through the funeral without knowing how, sensed her legs bearing her along, the hardness of the pew and the bodies pressed against hers. Work had given her a month off, just like that, and she was grateful. She thought fleetingly of the projects she had underway and the report that had been due the day after Winter's death. Then she pushed the thoughts away again.

Little by little, she began to roam around the house. She forced herself to pause beside the toys in the box, Winter's chair at the kitchen table, and the plastic mat in the living room, where he'd loved to sit and draw. At night she went to bed early with her iPad switched on. Winter's duvet, in which she lived and breathed, stopped smelling of him in the end. She had worn it out.

One Sunday evening, the first month had passed. The earth on the grave had begun to sink; rain and wind had buffeted the stone, which was no longer the newest in the churchyard.

"Come on," she said to Nala, who didn't want to jump down off the bed at first. "There we go, come on, we're leaving now."

And with gentle hands she removed the bedclothes, folded her son's duvet, turned the heating down low, and locked the door behind her.

A fallow deer ran through the garden that night. Elisabeth was standing by the garbage can when she heard it, having just thrown out the bedding. A rumbling, alien noise that was muffled by the grass. The animal stopped maybe ten metres from her. It stood there in the twilight with its head half turned away; it seemed to her she could hear it breathing. Neither of them moved. My little boy is dead, she thought. And I have condemned myself to keep living. Perhaps she was the first to stir, she wasn't sure, but abruptly the animal lurched into motion, flung itself sidelong, and careened away toward the forest.

CHAPTER TWO

September 2024

————

SHADI

"SHADI?"

The voice is much too loud for the concentrated silence of the reading room. Shadi is absorbed in a train of thought about grief as the dark side of love, and the interruption is like a slap to the head.

"You're Shadi, right?"

She swivels and shushes the girl, recognizing her immediately from her teaching group. Anna, that's her name. With her crop top and the vestiges of pink in her short hair, she looks like she came straight from a festival. Shadi has never really spoken to her, but she's got a pretty clear idea of who Anna is. She's the type who's stuck to the reading groups they were assigned by the teachers at the start of the course, because she enjoys having someone to discuss Simone de Beauvoir with until late into the night while she smokes roll-your-own cigarettes and takes a metaphorical hatchet to the patriarchy. The type who takes up too much time in class but forgets to study for exams.

Right now, she looks pretty worse for wear. Her eyes are bloodshot, and even at this distance Shadi thinks she can smell booze.

"Let's go outside," she whispers.

On the way out they're followed by the other students' scowls, and Shadi gets it. She hates it when someone breaks the imposed silence.

"Well?" she asks, once the door has closed.

"Isn't there anywhere we can sit down?" asks Anna, and Shadi leads her into the kitchenette. The chairs scrape across the battered concrete floor as they sit down.

"You know who I am, right?" continues Anna. Shadi nods. "Good. I've just been to see Thorsten about my dissertation, and it turns out I'm a bit late finding a supervisor. That means he can't fit me in, at least not by myself. But if I work with someone he's already accepted…"

The sentence is a hook baited with a slippery worm Shadi is loath to swallow. Avoiding Anna's gaze, she concentrates on the ring given her by Emil, twisting it around and around on her finger.

Anna sighs. "Okay. You're writing about grief, I'm writing about grief, and if we work together we can share Thorsten. I had him for undergrad, and he was the best supervisor I ever had."

"Sorry." Shadi manages to squeeze out the word. Luckily, she sounds more determined than she feels. "I write best on my own. Anyway, I've already started." She glances up at Anna, then swiftly drops her gaze. That look.

"What's your research topic?"

"I haven't fully decided yet." Shadi's legs change position under the table, although she's making an effort not to fidget. "It'll be something about looking at the reasons why they chose to introduce grief as a diagnosis despite all the opposition to it. And then discussing advantages and disadvantages, ethically and professionally and, like, pragmatically."

"Pragmatically?" Anna almost spits out the word. "What are you talking about?"

Shadi swallows, trying to find the right words. "Lots of people with grief disorder did get a diagnosis before; it was just PTSD or depression. Maybe it makes more sense to call it what it is. Plus, this way it's easier for people to get the right treatment."

"Perfect!" Anna throws out her arms. "Why don't we just make up a diagnosis for homelessness too, so we can help people find a place to live?"

Shadi doesn't dare tell her there's a diagnosis for that already, in the Z codes. "Some people really do fall apart," she mumbles.

"But that doesn't mean they're ill!" Anna's voice has taken on a metallic ring; there's something wild in her grey-blue eyes. "Maybe they were lonely, maybe they've lost someone before, or they're struggling with a whole load of other stuff on top of everything, and so it knocks them off their feet. Vulnerability and mental illness aren't the same thing, you know!"

"There, see," shrugs Shadi, standing up to make some space between them. "We don't even want to write about the same topic."

Anna rises too. She's taller than Shadi, and now that they're face-to-face, it strikes her that she's probably a couple of years older as well.

"Fine!" Anna doesn't look like she thinks anything is even remotely fine. "Have fun with your pragmatic project. Big fucking thanks for your help!"

Shadi lingers in the kitchen for another minute after Anna has gone, collecting herself. There's a whirring in her feet, as though she's just narrowly escaped being mown down. But on her way back to the reading room, she sees Anna again. She's leaning against the wall further down the corridor, talking on the phone, and at first Shadi can't hear what she's saying.

Then she raises her voice. "Well, that's why I got a doctor's note! I just don't get how you can let me fail that subject. These are people's lives you're ruining!"

Back in the reading room, Shadi lowers herself into her chair and tries to remember where she left off, but she's way too agitated. At that moment she notices an email has arrived from Thorsten. She skims it quickly, then shuts her eyes and lets her head sink backwards. So he was the one who recommended Anna come and find her. He says it would be a big help if Shadi would consider working with her. *Of course, you're well within your rights to say no,* he's added at the bottom, but that's not true. Her throat tightens. Not only does Anna hate her, but Shadi has unwittingly gone directly against her supervisor's wishes. She starts packing up her things mechanically: she won't get any more work done today anyway. If it's really so healthy to set boundaries, like everybody says, she thinks as she switches off the reading lamp, then why does it always feel so totally miserable?

THORSTEN

"AH, HELLO THERE." THORSTEN STEPS into the meeting room, where Elisabeth—head of research at Danish Pharma—is already in her seat. "Back again, I see?"

Elisabeth has been working as a consultant on the grief trial and has sat in on a couple of their meetings. This type of collaboration between the university and the industry is highly unusual, but it was one of the conditions Aarhus had to meet in order to obtain permission to study the new drug at such an early stage. Although Thorsten was initially against it, he's got to admit it's gone smoothly thus far.

Elisabeth looks up from her phone and nods. "I am indeed. Although I understand you're nearly done," she adds. "So for me this might be the last time."

Thorsten takes a seat a little way down the table. Elisabeth has sat at one end, and Kamilla, his boss, will definitely want the other.

"By the way, who was the young woman you were talking to earlier?" asks Elisabeth. "Tall, cropped hair, very passionate?" She nods toward the corridor, and at once her smile punctures the aura of almost exaggerated professionalism she normally radiates. "I borrowed the office next to yours for a couple of hours this morning. It was pretty difficult not to overhear you."

"Ah yes, that must have been Anna," says Thorsten. "One of my students. She can be a little loud. Always ready to argue, you know."

At that moment Kamilla enters with Cecilie and Svend. She heads straight to speak to Elisabeth, while Cecilie sets a cake tin on the table. Svend sits down beside Thorsten with a harassed expression on his face.

"Christ on a cracker," he snorts. "Every attempt to make a psychology student understand even a fraction of how the brain is put together is like teaching a bloody infant to play the saxophone."

Around them, the rest of the research group are finding their seats.

"Cake?" Cecilie hands Svend a plate. "It's been made with almond flour, so I'm afraid you can't eat it, Thorsten."

"That's a shame," he says, but when he gets a proper look at the mass of nuts and dried fruit Cecilie calls cake, he doesn't feel so bad about his allergies

"Good afternoon, everybody." Kamilla cuts through the small talk. "Lovely to see you. This is one of the last times the whole group will come together—" she nods first at Miguel, who is a consultant at Skejby Hospital, then to Jesper, chief psychologist at the National Centre for Grief "—so I imagine we'll spend the meeting today talking about the preliminary results Anton has brought for us. That's also why we've got Elisabeth back with us, in case there are any last questions to discuss."

She smiles at Elisabeth, then lets her gaze sweep across every single face around the table. "It's crucial that we come to a mutual understanding of what we have found here. Focus on Callocain will only increase in the coming months as it nears approval, and I hope our study will be a key contribution to an already very polarized debate."

There's nodding. Next to Thorsten, Svend is munching loudly on the sorry excuse for a cake.

"As you know, Anton has been working non-stop on his analysis." Kamilla gestures toward Anton, who is responsible for the statistical collation of the data Thorsten and the others have gathered. "These are the fruits of our labours and what we will base our articles on, so it's all very exciting. Anton, if you'd give us a rundown?"

Anton, whose last name is Maninnen and who apparently has Finnish roots, gets to his feet and passes around some handouts.

"As you're all aware, we have been testing a group of just under four hundred patients diagnosed with prolonged grief disorder," he begins. "Half were randomly selected to receive treatment with Callocain while the other half were given calcium tablets, and I think it's safe to say that we have found the same significant effect as Elisabeth and her team at Danish Pharma. Callocain had a significant to strong impact on up to 75 per cent of those who received the pills, and of course that's a respectable number compared to, say, the treatment of depression or schizophrenia."

Thorsten is watching Elisabeth while Anton talks. She is listening with a small smile but looks neither surprised nor relieved, he thinks. She looks like someone getting confirmation of what she already knows.

"In addition to the cognitive and personality assessments, our battery of tests consists of the grief screening itself, a two-part test focusing on empathy, and a series of PET scans to help build up an image of how participants in the trial recall their lost loved one. And it's in these scans that, in my opinion, we find one of the keys to the positive effect."

Anton enunciates each individual letter in PET, instead of saying it like the word *pet*, the way he's supposed to. He's a fairly new hire, loaned out to various departments on a project-by-project basis whenever someone needs assistance with stats, and it's the first time Thorsten has worked with him. His impression is that the numbers nerd is the type of employee worth his weight in gold but who wilts if he's dragged out into the light for too long.

"During the scans, we showed participants a series of neutral images of nature, strangers, and so on, interspersed with some private photographs of their loved one. You can see the results here." Anton leafs through a few pages in the handout and points. "The group on the medication simply reacted less to the images of their loved one than the control group did, in terms of both brain activity and pulse."

Thorsten looks at the two blocks and the dots dancing over the paper. Somewhere in these graphs are Birgit, Mikkel, and all the others he's tested. They lay in the vast belly of the PET scanner while the tracer circulated to those centres of the brain that were most active. The flow of blood through the various structures made them light up blue, yellow, and red, and Anton points at the images. He explains that, taken together, the scans offer a prototype of a grieving brain that's been given Callocain and a grieving brain that hasn't.

"As you can see, there is reduced activity in the relevant structures in a brain on Callocain. The amygdala and the hippocampus are especially interesting here, because they don't light up nearly as much as in the control group." Anton takes off his reading glasses. "In conclusion, we can say that the medicated group seems to remember their loved one less acutely, or at least in a less emotionally charged way. Basically, it's much less painful to remember them if you've taken the drug."

"Very interesting," says Kamilla, smiling at him. "Especially if you compare this to our other tests, which show no indication of general memory loss or other similar cognitive difficulties related to the pills."

Elisabeth bows her head in an almost imperceptible nod. "We have been lucky with our target," she says. "And of course I'm delighted your study supports the results we have already seen at Danish Pharma."

Their post-doc, Rikke, and a couple of the others launch into a discussion about the significance of cognitive impairments in grief-stricken people, and Thorsten's attention wanders. He flicks through the handout until he reaches the tests he helped conduct. The ups and downs of the curves stare back at him from the page. He's already looking forward to the detective work involved in understanding what they've actually found.

ANNA

ANNA STILL HASN'T HAD ANYTHING except Thorsten's scalding-hot coffee, so she buys a sandwich at the library cafeteria and wolfs it down at one of the tables. She has no idea what to do. Shadi made herself pretty clear, and Svend could barely be bothered to look up from his computer screen long enough to tell her she was the third dissertation student this week he'd said no to supervising. So close, and now the whole thing is slipping away. Why can't she ever hang on to anything?

As soon as she's stuffed the last bite into her mouth, she grabs her tray and steps directly out in front of a woman with a thick book under her arm and a full cup, the contents of which nearly spill.

"Hi." The woman smiles at Anna. Her hair is big and curly, and she seems almost to be shining, standing there in the café.

"Hi," answers Anna stupidly, and only then does the woman stand aside so she can move past.

"Unless you wanted to sit down for a bit?" She nods at the chair from which Anna has just risen.

It's not often someone flirts with her so overtly, at least not in daylight. And if she hadn't been so frustrated and things hadn't been such a gigantic mess, she would definitely have sat back down to see where things went.

"That's sweet of you," Anna says, "but I can't stay."

Minutes later she's cycling across town as fast as the creaking bike can carry her.

"You've got so thin, there's no muscle on you! Have you seen yourself?"

Isam is laughing at her. He lifts her tired right arm into the air and flicks her biceps.

She yanks it back. "All right, chill!"

He dances away, still grinning.

"I'm heading over to the bag."

She's got no energy left, but she needs to get back in shape, and plus he's right. She's lost weight, and her cardio is way worse too. The lactic acid doesn't even have time to build up in her legs before she's out of breath.

The first punches hit home. Precise, swift out and swift back; she could floor a man with blows like that. The yells of others fill the air around her, and the thick reek of sweat scorches her nose. She switches between jabs and hooks, whirls around and aims a hard kick into the side of the bag. How is she going to write the dissertation now? Does she really need to find a new topic? She kicks again.

"Keep going!" Isam appears beside her. "Come on, strike through!"

She can feel her technique slipping as the weariness eats into her muscles. Her feet skid in the drops of perspiration from her brow. Her knuckles sting. And then there's that whole fucking car crash with the neuro class she failed. As she left, Thorsten suggested she make a formal complaint, but that's easy for him to say. He has no idea what that would take.

"Watch your elbow," she hears Isam shout, and she knows he's right but doesn't have the energy to correct it. She keeps striking, forcing herself to continue, pushing her body until there's a ringing in her ears, and suddenly, she pitches forward over the blue mat and heaves up the contents of her stomach in hard, sour thrusts.

"For fuck's sake!" She can just make out Isam on the periphery of her vision, his round face twisted with disgust. "You can clean that up yourself."

He disappears toward a group of young, gawking onlookers. Anna stands there with her hands on her knees, spitting into the puddle before her while her diaphragm contracts in churning shudders.

SHADI

THE CUCUMBER IS FROM YESTERDAY, but Shadi gives it a sniff, cautiously pinching the green skin. Satisfied, she cuts it in half and sprinkles it with salt before settling down on the sofa. From here she can look out over the sea, where the gusting wind makes it look like a giant squid is on the seabed, shooting ink up toward the surface.

She's staying home today, and stacks of books are waiting for her on the kitchen table. Although they were only officially supposed to start writing their dissertations a week and a half ago, she got underway ages before that. Anna touched a nerve when she asked about her thesis, but Shadi knows pretty much what she wants to write about, and when the idea first came to her last year it had seemed exciting and, she thought, important. Now she's on the brink of it, she mainly just thinks of the dissertation as a jumbled heap of disconnected letters that need to be meticulously sorted and moved from one pile into another.

The cucumber is gone, and she can't procrastinate any longer. She decides to persevere with her outline of the diagnosis. The original English term is *prolonged grief disorder*, which she prefers to the Danish *persistent*. Who would want a persistent disorder if they could settle for a prolonged one? She drums her fingers against the keyboard. Should she go through all the diagnostic criteria one by one, or is it enough to give a superficial account? She'll have to ask Thorsten when she sees him at the next supervision. For now she'll content herself with noting that losing and missing a loved one is the primary component of the disorder, and what distinguishes it from, say, depression.

As always, she saves the document repeatedly as she writes, but she still doesn't feel entirely safe. Things vanish, screens can go black, and then all is lost. This stuff happens. Stop it, she admonishes herself as she uploads it to Dropbox for the second time. It's saved now. But she can't help it.

In her first semester they'd had Social and Individual Psychology, and in the seminar—run by a precocious PhD student—they had all taken a personality test to experience the theory first-hand. The teacher had explained that there was no such thing as good or bad test scores, but of course there was. A high neuroticism score, for example, was associated with mental illness and premature death. Openness, in which Shadi rated catastrophically low, was one of the parameters everyone loved, while nobody envied her the trait she scored spectacularly well in. Everybody knew what conscientiousness meant, and that was exactly how they saw her. Practical, square, boring.

On the other hand, she thinks, opening the document she has created for references and suggestions for further reading, it's precisely those qualities that mean she'll be leaving the psychological institute with one of the highest averages in her graduating class.

"Hey, sweetheart!"

Emil is a wave of energy streaming into the apartment, although she can tell from his voice that he's tired. She goes into the kitchen, where he's busy emptying a shopping bag onto the table.

"How's it going here?" he asks, giving her a kiss. "Anything new from your hungover dissertation friend?"

Shadi knows she has a habit of making her life at university more interesting than it really is. One time she made up a bonkers wrong number purely to make Emil laugh, and she might have laid it on a bit thick yesterday when she told him about her run-in with Anna. "She texted earlier, actually," she says, taking the bag of tomatoes out of Emil's hands. She starts rinsing them one by one under the cold tap. "But I haven't replied yet."

"Oh yeah? What did she want?" Emil is chopping up a red onion with soft, assured movements.

Shadi switches off the water and goes to stand behind him. She presses her cheek against the hollow between his shoulder blades, which feel as though they were made just for her, and tries to let her breathing fall in line with his. "She wants to meet. Says she has something that will change my mind. What do you reckon, is it a trap?"

His laughter is a deep growl against her cheek. "It's most definitely a trap," he says. "You need to watch out for that one, love. She's dangerous!"

July 2011

ELISABETH

ELISABETH HAD SHOVED WINTER THROUGH his bedroom door and shut it securely, but she could still wind time neither forward nor back. How did you find meaning again when it had lived in another person, and that person was lost? That was how it felt. She lost her child. And since it was Winter who brought substance to her hours and made her carry out an apparently endless stream of movements, day in and day out, she was now left directionless. All the softness she had found in herself had been for him. The care with which she had held his little body when she bathed him as an infant, the tenderness with which she had combed his fair hair and breathed in his velvety cheeks, had been made homeless, and without him her former hardness returned threefold. It was that or total collapse.

The movements remained in her body, and from the outside they must have looked largely the same. Getting up, taking a shower, eating breakfast, setting off for work. Her practised lips shaped themselves around vowels and consonants, her fingers brought forth shimmering strings of numbers and letters designed to lead her onward, forward. But inside, it was obvious. All direction was missing.

When she came home late after yet another long day, Nala bounded up to her, so happy that her whole chubby body wagged with glee. Most days, Elisabeth paid the girl next door a small fortune to avoid having to deal with the dog. All she could think of when she saw it was her absent son.

"Down!" she ordered, but she had to repeat it three or four times before the dog, after one last warm lick of her hand, gave up and trotted back to its basket. There it lay down, while Elisabeth flitted restlessly. Often she'd drink a glass of wine, sometimes washing down an Advil or two, and told herself it was her reward for having ground through yet another day. Other times she went for a run. That worked too, and the more kilometres she put behind her, the easier it was to fall asleep. But why she was fighting to stay alive, why she didn't just give up—that she didn't even know herself.

One Saturday she drove down to the local charity shop to drop off Winter's clothes. She placed the black bags just inside the door and waved apologetically to the woman at the counter before hurrying back out. His toys she gave to friends and friends of friends, and in the end, she threw out what was left.

Her favourite photographs, the one from his first birthday and the one from nursery, where his soft face was starting to take shape, were allowed to stay up in his room. That was still where she sought refuge when the loss got too intense. Whenever she unlocked the door, Nala would squeeze past her with an eager whine, as if she thought Winter had hidden from them inside. The dog searched every corner painstakingly with her damp snout, until finally she stared up at Elisabeth, confused. Now Winter was at once everywhere and nowhere at all.

CHAPTER THREE

September 2024

THORSTEN

ARRIVING AT THE OFFICE IN the morning, Thorsten sends the portrait of his old mentor a nod, as always. He took it himself at Hudson's farewell lecture, and now it hangs above the sofa as a reminder of the late professor's credo: never put the system before the human being. Always see the individual as a goal in itself. Unfortunately, the downside of the photograph is that it also reminds Thorsten of better times, when there was less admin and much more immersion in actual practice—at least, that's how he remembers it.

He still hasn't heard a peep from Mikkel, the no-show from the other day, even though Thorsten has called several times and left yet another message. And maybe it's Hudson, glaring sharp-eyed on the wall, but the first thing he does that morning is scan his contact list and dial the number belonging to Mikkel's sister.

"This is Louise," says a voice at the other end.

Thorsten introduces himself and explains why he's calling. Since the sister took part in Mikkel's introductory session way back at the inception of the project, it doesn't feel like too much of a violation of confidentiality.

"This is a fragile group of people we're dealing with here," he says, "so I always try to get in touch when someone doesn't show up."

"He has been pretty hard to get hold of recently," says Louise. "I've been wondering whether it's too difficult for him to be with me and the kids, now that he's alone. I mean, he's never said it aloud, but it could be that, don't you think?"

There's something touching about her sincerity, and Thorsten agrees it sounds plausible. "But apart from that you haven't noticed anything different lately?" he inquires. "It could be anything. His interests, his mood, something about his demeanour that's changed?"

"Well, he quit the football club where he was a youth coach. That was actually one of the few things he clung on to after the accident. He's been there more than ten years."

Thorsten scribbles the answer on his notepad. Mikkel hasn't mentioned that. "But it doesn't seem to you like he's getting upset or sad again?"

"Recently? No, I don't think so," replies Louise. "Maybe a bit short-tempered, you know, but for the most part he's actually in a surprisingly good mood." Then she grasps what Thorsten is driving at. "You don't think something's happened to him?"

"No, no," says Thorsten quickly. "I don't think anything. I just like to wrap things up properly."

That seems to reassure her, and she promises to ask her brother to call as soon as she hears from him.

Thorsten is in the middle of preparing for dinner that night when he hears the distinctive Skype jingle coming from the computer. Must be Andreas. They've largely kept to their weekly chats, but last time the signal was so bad they had to give up.

"Just a minute," he says, after clicking the green handset on the screen. The air in the kitchen is thick with the smell of cooking, so he quickly cracks open the window and switches off the gas, although he's only just put the meat in the pan. Then he sits down in the living room with his computer in front of him.

"Hi, Dad."

Andreas looks happy and faraway over the scratchy connection. He's got such long hair now that he can gather it into a ponytail. The conversation begins a little haltingly, but they're still better than they were in the beginning; somehow they've found their rhythm. And much as Thorsten hates to admit it, he talks to his son more now that he's travelling around Asia than when he was home in Aarhus.

"I'm moving on tomorrow," Andreas tells him. "With someone I met on a hike the other day."

"Oh yeah?" Thorsten had thought he was staying in Guilin for a while, but Andreas's plans change all the time. "Have you packed?"

Andreas laughs, making the line crackle. "This is literally everything I have, Dad." He turns the screen and pats the backpack that's resting against the wall. "All the crap people pick up back home—" he shakes his head "—it's all filler, the lot of it. Just think of your basement. I have everything I need right here."

Thorsten can't help but smile. Each generation rebels in its own way. That's probably as it should be—hairstyle and idealism included.

"There's plenty of your stuff in that basement too, you know," he says, "from when you were little. Maybe we can look through it together one day."

It feels like a whole lifetime ago that Anita packed the car, buckled a pale Andreas into the back seat, and set off for her new home in Åbyhøj. A new-build terraced house with exposed beams. She'd said so when she told Thorsten about her plan, for God's sake, as though the exposed beams were even remotely relevant when she was leaving him after fifteen years together.

"What about the piano?" Andreas asks. "Have you still got that?"

"Of course."

Thorsten remembers precisely where they put it: up against the far wall, to the right of the window. He still remembers the pressure behind his eyeballs, the day Andreas hissed that he hated the stupid hunk of junk, that he didn't want to visit anymore if he was going to be forced to play it.

"I miss you," says Thorsten, and whatever anyone might say, Andreas definitely gets that smile from him.

"Same here," Andreas says, and he holds out his hand as though the screen were a window, and they were separated not by thousands of miles but only by a sheet of glass. When Thorsten does the same, it's almost as though they can reach.

SHADI

IT WAS ANNA'S IDEA TO meet at a café in the city centre instead
of the library. Shadi hates cafés. Way too many people crammed
into way too little space; it's impossible to know what the hygiene
level is like in the kitchen, and the whole process of interacting
with a waiter is a humiliation she'd rather avoid.

"So," she says, after Anna has gone up to order, "there was
something you wanted to show me?"

But Anna leans back, balancing the chair on two legs, and
gives her an appraising stare from behind half-lowered lids. "First,
you tell me what you got in clinical psychology last year."

Shadi feels like snapping that it's none of her business. On the
other hand, everyone knows Thorsten's stingy with marking, especially in that subject, where a ten from him is the same as a twelve
from most of the others.

"Ten."

"Ha!" exclaims Anna, landing back on all four legs of the chair.
"There's your first reason to work with me. I know exactly how
Thorsten works—we're like this." She demonstrates, crossing her
middle and index fingers.

"So it was you who got that twelve?"

A rumour had gone around the group that one of them had
managed to wring a top mark out of Thorsten, but it had never
occurred to her that it could be Anna.

"It was. I also had him as a supervisor for my undergrad thesis.
He spent more time with me than he had to, got hold of a spe-
cialist in Canada and all sorts of things. I got a twelve for that too.
Not that I'm super into the whole grade thing—I just got a two in
developmental psych. But I feel like it matters a bit more to you."

At that moment the waiter arrives with their food. Anna
immediately takes a huge bite of her veggie burger, squelching red
cabbage and tomato everywhere, and within a few seconds she's
smeared in guacamole. There's something overwhelming about her,
regardless of whether she's angry, like the other day, or in a good

mood, like right now. As though she's actively trying to provoke some kind of reaction.

"Maybe it does," is all Shadi can come up with. This whole thing is backwards. From a distance, letting Anna in on her project had reeked of pity, but it might actually end up being to her advantage. So far, she hasn't seen even a sliver of the enthusiasm from Thorsten that Anna is talking about. He's every bit as capable as she expected, but friendly in such a distanced way that she suspects he's forgotten her name the second she's out the door. At the same time, the grade thing is infuriating, and she feels like asking about Anna's average simply to restore the proper order. Trouble is, she believes what Anna says. She genuinely doesn't care.

Shadi prods at the food. The avocado is tasteless, and so hard it's difficult to get it down, but can she allow herself to pick it out? Gingerly she coaxes out a slice.

"What's up?" asks Anna.

"Nothing. It's just the avocado, it's not super ripe."

Anna reaches over and jabs the piece with her fork. "Ask for a new one."

"Nah, it's fine, I'm just getting the worst of it out." After a little more digging, she finds another lump and nudges it to the edge of the plate.

"Seriously?"

Before she can react, Anna has called over the waiter. "We'd like another sandwich, please, if you've got a ripe avocado," she says, pointing at Shadi's side of the table. "That one's hard as a rock."

Shadi can't bring herself to meet the waiter's eyes. But ten minutes later, just as Anna is about to present what she calls her fantastic, almost incredible thesis, she's given a new sandwich with a glass of juice as an apology.

"Thanks," she mumbles, not quite sure whether she's addressing Anna or the waiter.

ANNA

IN A FIT OF ENTHUSIASM, Anna takes a book about the two-track model of bereavement counselling into the kitchen after her run and starts reading while she stretches. The world is open once again. After her conversation with Thorsten the other day she was ready to give up: now she's Anna, who's going to write her dream dissertation with her favourite supervisor. Yeah, she's got Shadi in tow, but if that's the price, she's more than willing to pay it. It gives her exactly the plan she was missing. A clearly delineated time span with a finishing line in five and a half months, when they have to hand it in.

Still out of breath, she takes a few gulps straight from the tap, then changes legs so she can stretch her other thigh. Grief must be understood as a pendulum, she reads, swinging between the agony of the loss and avoidance coping, which seeks to protect the self from intense emotion. Yawn. The authors call one the loss-oriented process and the other the restorative, and she really should look up *restorative* to make sure she knows what it means. Then, like lightning, it happens. It's always been a problem, and it's only got worse in recent years. The stiff, academic language knocks the wind out of her.

Frustrated, she slams the book shut and goes to Wikipedia instead. At least that's comprehensible. "Grief as a diagnosis first appeared in the USA in 2013, in an appendix to their manual, the DSM, while the WHO's ICD series didn't introduce it as a psychiatric diagnosis until 2018," she reads. Prolonged grief disorder was first translated and introduced to Denmark in the early 2020s, but when she googles it, she finds newspaper articles dating all the way back to 2014. Most take a negative slant, with headlines like "The Sick Dark Side of Love" and "Healing on Prescription." A feature published last year in the *Kristeligt Dagblad* is more moderate, talking about people who want to be rid of difficult challenges but risk losing their ethical compass along the way. Anna smiles to herself. This has got to be the first time she's ever agreed with that newspaper.

One calf is beginning to cramp up, so she puts down her phone and does a lap around the flat. Back in the kitchen, she peers into the gapingly empty fridge. For a moment she considers if she's up to doing a quick shop, but she also needs a shower, and it's so much easier to just call Milan on the corner and order the usual.

Once that's done, a notification pings in from Hinge. At first she can't place the person who appears onscreen, but then she realizes: it's the woman from before, the one she nearly bumped into in the library cafeteria. Siri, her name is. Her curls are up in a bun, the picture is probably a couple of years old, and she's gazing earnestly, almost arrogantly, back at Anna. If you want me, says the gaze, then take your best shot. She's a bit older than Anna would usually go for, but she sends a heart back anyway.

Her own profile picture is the one from last year's Midsummer's Eve where she's sitting on the beach, squinting in the sun with a beer in her hand. She looks happy, and if she thinks back, maybe she was. Happier, at any rate.

A few hours later, having added yet another pizza box to the tower in the kitchen and hung her damp running clothes in their usual spot over the backs of the chairs, she flings herself onto the bed. Her dad has called three times in the past week and left a single, helpless message, but she's in no mood to talk to him. It's not that they've fallen out. She just gets upset with him so quickly, and then she'll feel bad all over again. She ends up sending a short text promising to call one of these days.

Just as she's about to put down the phone, it lights up again.

Want to meet up? Like for real?

It's from Siri.

SHADI

EMIL DIDN'T SAY WHEN HE was coming home, and as seven o'clock approaches, Shadi can't do any more work. Her eyes are sore from hours glued to the screen, so she saves the dissertation, which is growing with reassuring speed, and blinks once or twice to get rid of the dryness. Then she gets dinner on. She slices a pat of butter into a saucepan with some pasta, chops parsley, and sprinkles on some lemon zest to finish. But Emil still hasn't come, and by the time his key finally slips into the lock, her plate has been empty for ages.

"Sorry, I'm a bit later than I thought." He comes over to her in the living room. His nose is cold against hers. "Hey, you're not angry, are you?"

She shrugs. Minutes later she can hear him drinking a glass of water, then he's standing beside her again.

"Why don't you ever listen to your records?" he asks.

"Huh? I do."

"No you don't. It's always dead silent when I come home." He lifts the lid on the record player. "This one's been on here since forever."

Shadi draws her knees up to her chest and folds her arms around them. "Well, I'm busy. I can't concentrate if there's music on."

Emil mutters something. He drops the lid and flips restlessly through the pile of records.

"Aren't you hungry?" she asks, getting to her feet.

"I've eaten."

"Oh." There's a crackling in her head. "With who? You could have told me."

Emil whirls toward her, moving so quickly that Shadi freezes in the middle of the room. "So, I should have asked for permission first, is that it?"

She shakes her head, unease streaking out of her chest and down her arms. She doesn't understand what's going on. If this had been a normal evening, she would have told Emil about how excessive vegetable consumption was once considered a sign of mental illness, or he would have grumbled about some new computer system they had to use at work. They'd have sat on the sofa and ate pomelos, and later they'd have found a movie on Netflix. Instead, he looks to be spoiling for a fight.

"If I'd called," he says, "we both know what would have happened, don't we? You'd have been all sad and I'd have felt guilty, though I did anyway, of course. And then I'd have ended up cycling home straight away. Again!"

The last word is almost a shout. Something alien and dangerous has got wedged between them, and Shadi remembers what she normally forgets. That she doesn't see everything about Emil. That things happen inside him she knows nothing about.

"What do you want?" He throws up his hands. "Am I supposed to apologize because I went out to eat with my colleagues?"

"No," she mumbles. "I just think you could have let me know, that's all." Her thudding heart pushes her back down onto the sofa. She shouldn't say the next thing, she knows that. "And I don't get why you'd rather be with them than with me."

He looks dumbfounded. "What are you talking about? Of course I wouldn't."

She should have just been happy with that, she should have stopped right there. Her chin quivers, she has to press her fingers to her mouth, yet the words cannot be held back. "Then why do you go out with them instead of coming home to eat with me? I mean, you've been with them all day."

"Honestly, Shadi." Emil exhales, as though dealing with some utterly exhausting thing. "Do you seriously never want to hang out with anyone except me?"

"No," she says defiantly, but he tilts his head and drags out the silence until it becomes pointed.

"I think you're holding yourself back," he says at last. "You're the cleverest, loveliest person I know, but nobody's allowed to see it. Isn't that right, Shadi?"

Later he opens the bedroom door, where she's lying on the bed. Her head feels heavy, and full of something she can't get out. For some reason she still hasn't cried.

"You want to go out?" he asks.

"For a walk?"

He nods.

It's drizzling, so she pulls on her thick winter jacket, winding her scarf around the collar. Emil waits as she zips up her boots. She wobbles on one leg and feels ungainly when she reaches out for the wall.

He lets her go ahead so he can lock the door after them, twisting the handle three times for her sake, even though he thinks it's dumb. You can spend your whole life saying thank you and sorry, she thinks, repeating the same patterns, saying the same words with a little less care each time, while the other person finds it harder and harder to hear them.

As they walk the first few metres along the pavement, their hands find each other in the waterlogged dark.

August 2011

ELISABETH

SEVERAL PEOPLE SUGGESTED ELISABETH *talk to someone*—they each came up with a different name, all of them apparently having seen a therapist at some point—or that she take part in one of the support groups organized by the council. She couldn't imagine anything worse.

"Maybe it's all been a bit too fast," said Malene when she dropped by one day. "You think you're doing better, but it seems more like you've just put a lid on everything." She looked around. "And where have all your things gone?"

What a ridiculous image, thought Elisabeth. *Putting a lid on everything*. It sounded like something inside her was about to boil over, as though in seconds it would be bubbling underneath the lid, squeezing out droplets that ran down the sides and evaporated in sizzling pops. But it wasn't like that at all. There was no volcano, no burning pain, only barrenness and futility like she'd never known before.

"My friend went to a group after she lost her mom," Malene continued. "She found it really helpful. It might be easier for you to talk about Winter in that environment—with people who don't already know you."

There might be something to that. It was virtually impossible for Elisabeth to talk to the people around her about Winter. She was afraid they'd start to cry, that they'd tell her their own stories of loss or burden her with their private memories of Winter. It was hard enough to bear her own.

"Thanks, that's sweet of you," she replied, hoping Malene would be leaving soon. "I'll look into it."

She did not, in fact, have any intention of going through with it, but that night Malene sent her a link to a support group for people who had lost loved ones. They called it an open group, because you could start and finish whenever you liked, and two days later, to her own surprise, Elisabeth found herself pressed up against the wall of the churchyard where her son lay buried, staring across at a brightly lit room on the other side of the road. From her hiding place in the shadow of a big tree, she watched car after car pull up outside and drop people off. People who looked exactly like everybody else.

Inside, the chairs were arranged in a circle, and when Elisabeth finally steeled herself to cross the street, there were still seats free. She didn't know how you were supposed to act in places like this, but caught the eye of a red-haired woman. They exchanged nods.

"Welcome. Is this your first time?" A man in his fifties appeared beside her and introduced himself as the group leader, and on a sudden impulse, Elisabeth gave her middle name instead of her first. There was something mad about the whole thing, about the trolley cart of plastic cups and the hideous lino and the way they all slipped so effortlessly into their roles. Grieving people were good people, it seemed. Grieving people smiled compassionately at each other and spoke in subdued voices.

As the hour struck, the group leader welcomed them. The rules were simple. You put up your hand when you had something to say, you listened, and beyond that you stuck to your lane. Crossing her legs, Elisabeth tried to remind herself that here she could be anyone at all.

It was the red-haired woman who spoke. She had evidently been before, and when she talked there was something rote about it, as though she'd practised the words at home.

"I'm trying to make the days pass," she explained. "The two little ones have to go to school, my husband's off to work. It's all continuing around me somehow." She looked up from her hands, which were tightly folded in her lap. "I replay it all the time, that day on the beach when Lucas drowned. We'll be sitting in the middle of dinner, one of the kids will be telling me something that happened on the playground, and suddenly I realize I'm some-where else altogether. That somehow I got stuck on that beach, while the rest of my family…"

"No." Elisabeth flinched. She hadn't meant to say anything; the word had just slipped out of her mouth. All eyes were now fixed on her. "I'm sorry," she said, getting to her feet. "I'd better go."

The group leader put up a good fight, though. She was welcome to stay without saying anything, she was welcome to come back any time if she changed her mind, this space was just as much hers as anyone else's. But that wasn't true. Elisabeth could feel it in every single cell: she didn't belong here either. She didn't even fit among the mourners, and moments later she was back outside, her eyes shamefully dry.

But though she never went back to the group, the meeting had caused something to shift. Perhaps because she saw how many others were like her, pecked and eaten by the birds of loss. Searching online, she found that roughly 55,000 people died in Denmark every year. Each and every one of them seemed part of a vast net, like the toy cobwebs she and Winter had made out of matchsticks and chestnuts in the autumn. Each match head represented a life that had changed forever, now that the dead person was gone. Mothers, fathers, siblings, friends, teachers, colleagues, boyfriends, girlfriends, grandparents, spouses, and children. So many holes punched in so many lives, so easily. It must have been then that the idea first popped into her head.

CHAPTER FOUR

September 2024

ANNA

ANNA COUNTS SEVENTEEN PIZZA BOXES, which she tramples until they're flat enough for the recycling bin. The sun is beating down through the leaves. They're still green on several of the trees in the square, but soon they will yellow and twirl toward the asphalt, settling in the puddles and sticking to her boots when she fetches her bike. She pauses, her head turned to the east, and lets the light and the mild heat wrap around her body.

Her dad called again yesterday. She knows what an effort it is for him, but she sat there staring at the display while the three letters filled the screen. That's how it is these days: she pushes him out of her way like fresh, heavy snow; but of course, they can't go on like this. She takes her phone out of her pocket. Today is the kind of day when this seems possible.

"Anna," he says, and doesn't introduce himself like he often does, out of old habit from the days when phones didn't tell you who was calling.

"Hi, Dad."

As always, he asks how things are going, but he sounds different. She tells herself she sounds the same as usual, but really it's impossible to know. Neither of them is the same as before.

"Fine," she replies. "I've found a supervisor for my dissertation, and I'm going to write it with someone else from my year."

He doesn't say it's been too long since he saw her last. That he has no idea what she's been doing for the past few months. He doesn't ask if she's gone travelling without telling him or got drunk every night and fucked a bunch of random strangers to forget what happened last spring. Maybe he's not thinking that at all.

"How about you?" she asks.

"Ah, not much. I've been to the doctor."

"Yeah?"

"We're keeping me on sick leave from work for the time being. I haven't really..." He hesitates. "I don't think I'm quite ready to go back yet."

He knows perfectly well her opinion on all this. Even when he first went on sick leave, she said she didn't think it was a good idea to isolate himself like that. Wouldn't it be better to get back on the horse? Now he's vanished down exactly the rabbit hole she was afraid of, and she finds it hard to see how he will ever be able to return to his job, re-join the ranks of his old colleagues, and get his rhythm back. He's been at Sandkvist Electric for as long as she can remember, and she doubts he's ever considered anything else.

"How do you pass the time, then? Have you tidied up?"

She regrets the question as soon as the words are out. Why does it feel like she's wounding him every time they speak? She wishes desperately that she could be different, but round, soft words are a bad fit in her mouth.

"I've started making lists," he says, with a forced cheeriness that only makes her sadder. It's for her sake that he's making so much effort.

"Lists?"

"Yes, it was my doctor's suggestion. Every night I write out a list of things I'd like to do the following day, just little things. And then when I wake up, I look at it and know what I'm supposed to be doing. Then you cross things out when you've done them."

She pictures him by the kitchen table with his forehead creased in concentration, diligently writing *take the garbage out* on a lined notepad in his clumsy handwriting. The dust is descending around him, settling undisturbed on the shelves, the windowsills; there is no sound in the apartment. Then he switches off the light and gets into the big, empty bed.

"I'll come and visit soon, Dad," she says. "Next week, okay? I'll be there."

THORSTEN

"AND THAT IS WHY, MY young friends, the ability to build good relationships is by far your most important tool. No matter what approach you end up subscribing to, no matter what your clients are complaining about or how scintillating you might be..." There's scattered laughter in the hall. "If you don't build a solid rapport with them, the whole thing will fall flat."

The lecture is going well. The new students are always quiet at the beginning of the semester—only one of them dared to raise her hand—but a couple of them come down to speak to Thorsten afterwards, and he loves that. In recent years there has been steadily less time for this sort of thing and steadily more focus on obscure admin, not to mention a virtual assembly-line approach to the production of articles. Psychology may not be nearly as badly affected as some of the purely humanistic subjects, but the budget cuts haven't gone unnoticed, and ever since last year when they fired Puk, one of the most talented researchers Thorsten has ever known, he's been thinking that they must have hit rock bottom. But he still insists on making time for genuine communication with the students. Otherwise, they might as well fire him too.

Once the last few have left the auditorium, he goes back to his office and finds Anton's handout. On page eight are the images of brains, which strike him as simultaneously brilliant and massively oversimplified. No one has ever managed to put forward a coherent explanation of what goes on behind the walls of the skull: how the mind creates and preserves the memories that give us the impression of being the same person over time. For the most part, consciousness is still a riddle, and yet here he is, holding a meaningful depiction of the pain of loss. It really is miraculous.

The difference between the two brains on the page is so obvious that even a child would be able to point out the preponderance of yellows, greens, and blues in one scan as compared to the warmer reds and oranges in the other. The colours tell him that there was less blood flow to the brains of the subjects who had been given

Callocain when they were shown a photograph of their dead loved ones. Sounds simple enough—but what does it mean? That Callocain somehow dulls people's mental faculties, making them less sensitive? It strikes him instinctively as an unpleasant thought.

But since it's the interpersonal part, the empathy, that he's been most involved in, this is also where he needs to get a grip on the results. In any case, it's what he finds most immediately startling. He's read several studies about how grieving people sometimes rate lower than normal in terms of compassion and social activity, because they need to withdraw for a while. So far, so good. But surely logic would suggest that this tendency fades as people get better? He takes a sip of lukewarm coffee. Yet now he's staring at four columns that are all around the same height. Before treatment began and again six months later, across all the participants in the study. No significant change in empathy. The average score actually fell slightly in the group that was given Callocain, which is even harder to understand. Why on earth would someone become *less* compassionate toward others as their own pain faded into the background? Shouldn't a young man like Mikkel, who had been doing so much better, also find his ability to empathize with others restored?

He fishes out Mikkel's case notes from his folder of test results. It must be possible to dig a little deeper than Anton's overview allows. Thorsten has a rough sense of the numbers already, of course, but the results are still new to him. When you test nearly two hundred people using precisely the same questions, it's hard to avoid the whole process becoming a tad mechanical. Thorsten focused on creating a comfortable atmosphere, noting the participants' answers and drawing a circle around the number of points he feels they ought to give. All the work of doing random samples, totalling all the numbers, working out the individual scores and putting them in context he confidently left for Natasha, their PhD student. And Anton, of course.

Now he's looking at Mikkel's answers as though for the first time. Working through the points he has given him while painstakingly adding them up. Half an hour later, by the time he's gone through the whole thing not once but twice, he leans back in his chair with the papers in front of him. Taking off his glasses, he rubs his tired eyes. Can this really be true? In the final grief assessment, Mikkel scored only a four, which is a fantastic result. Clinically speaking, he doesn't even meet the diagnostic criteria for persistent grief anymore: he's cured. But it's the empathy score that really makes Thorsten's head spin. While the grief test gives a higher score the more symptoms you have, the empathy test rewards signs of compassion and interest in others, and as a personal rule of thumb he considers anything under ten to be a red flag. When he adds up Mikkel's answers, he comes up with only five points in the final round of testing. That's a big drop compared to the first time Thorsten spoke to him, which in itself is disconcerting. But that's not all. The score is so low that it's approaching the level you'd expect from someone with dissocial personality disorder—a diagnosis that not so very long ago was known as psychopathy.

SHADI

"I'm sure she'll be here soon," says Shadi, checking her phone again. No texts from Anna. Thorsten pours her some water and she takes the glass, devoid of anything even remotely intelligent to say. Instead, she takes a sip, swallowing much too loudly.

"So, making headway?" Thorsten gives her a smile. He doesn't seem to be aware of how awkward this is for her.

"Yeah, I think so. I'm up to fifteen pages," Shadi says. Then, to her own dismay, she starts listing all the articles she's read so far. "Andersen, Carson, Davidsen, Erikson et al.," she recites—she can't stop herself, "and Guldin has a great point about the way our concept of grief has developed historically, which—"

At that moment Anna comes bursting through the door in a flurry of cold air, cheeks still flushed from her bike ride.

"Sorry," she says, plopping onto the sofa beside Shadi. "What've I missed?"

"We've covered quite a lot of ground," says Thorsten, winking at Shadi. "But I think we're ready to move on to a more general conversation about where you're going with this thesis. Would you agree, Shadi?"

Somehow she manages to nod. Then she sinks back into the cushion and listens to Anna, who has no trouble putting her ideas into words. She watches her hands, which are either waving eagerly around in the air or banging the table to emphasize a point. She can't be sure, of course—there are limits to what we know about ourselves—but Shadi feels like when she talks, her own hands rest in her lap like wing-clipped birds.

"Are we seriously saying—" Anna looks appealingly from Thorsten to Shadi and back "—that even grief, one of the most basic human emotions, needs to be pathologized? If so, then the problem isn't people who are grieving. It's everybody else."

That old chestnut, thinks Shadi. Anna's going to flog that the whole way through the dissertation, until nobody can claim anymore that it's a nuanced viewpoint. Her top is clinging to her skin

underneath her sweater. If she's not careful, her breathing will start
to settle into an ache at the top of her chest.

"You guys do need to come up with your own take on the
material," Thorsten nods. "Grief as an inevitable part of being
human, and the ethical consequences of treating it as a psychiatric condition, that's certainly germane!" He throws out his arms. "I
mean, you could argue that loving someone and grieving their loss
when they die is one of the most significant responsibilities we will
ever face in our lives. Should we really be rushing it?"

"Exactly!" Anna exclaims.

Shadi takes a deep breath, shifting in her seat. It's not that
she disagrees, per se, but she's worried this approach is too one-
dimensional. Plus, she's going to be the one stuck with Anna when
the meeting ends. But then, luckily, Thorsten says something Shadi
would have said herself if she could.

"You need to play devil's advocate too, of course. This diagnosis,
these specific criteria—they haven't been plucked out of thin air.
There are many years of research behind them."

"Yeah, and an industry full of expert lobbyists and money
changing hands under the table," says Anna.

Thorsten guffaws. "There are several excellent arguments
for describing persistent grief as a psychiatric disorder, actually,"
he says. "And let's not forget that a diagnosis can help prevent
overtreatment."

"What do you mean?" asks Anna. "I'd have thought it was the
other way around."

"Without a diagnosis, there's a risk that everybody who's
bereaved will be offered a course of therapy," explains Thorsten,
"and that simply isn't necessary; most people can get through the
normal grieving process just fine with the help of their support
network. A diagnosis can help identify the relatively small group of
people who genuinely do need a hand."

"But do we really need a diagnosis for that?" asks Anna. "Isn't
that the sort of thing we're trained to evaluate?"

Thorsten shakes his head. "In my experience, we tend to let our therapeutic zeal run away with us. The way things are now, anyone with a dead relative can get subsidized therapy on the national health service. And not all of our colleagues keep up with the current literature—there are bound to be some of them who think sessions with a counsellor are always a plus."

Shadi's old therapist Annemette pops into her head. One day, nearly two years ago, she had shaken Shadi's hand and said it was time she stood on her own two feet. If she hadn't made that decision, Shadi would have kept going for sure. As exposed as she had felt talking about herself and all her weird thoughts, and despite the nerves every time she went, it had been nice, sitting there in Annemette's office. Nice to find someone other than Emil who she didn't have to hide from.

"I've met so many bereaved people who are in a terrible state," continues Thorsten. "People whose lives have completely ground to a halt. And when you're standing there in front of them, the idea that they're ill doesn't seem so far-fetched."

Shadi nods. Thorsten is right, they do exist. She's seen the statistics. And she knows from her own experience how powerful it can be to put a name to the thing you're struggling with.

"But is feeling bad really that dangerous?" Anna persists. "This is some *Matrix* shit, just taking a blue pill and forgetting the whole thing!"

Thorsten nods. He's clearly eating up everything Anna has to say. But that's the easy way out. Go vegan, cuddle pigs, love each other, and let life fall apart when tragedy strikes; it's all so easy to say when it doesn't cost you anything. "It's not that simple," says Shadi. At first she isn't sure the other two have even heard her. But there's silence in the room now, and when she looks up, both Thorsten and Anna are gazing at her expectantly "Mental illness does exist," Shadi says. "And I don't think there's anything particularly good or authentic about going to pieces if you can help it." She drops her eyes again. "Sometimes people just need help."

As soon as the meeting finishes, Shadi starts to pack up her things. She's had enough. Thorsten is gesticulating with a book by Robert Nozick; he and Anna are deep in conversation about dystopian cult stories. The snarl of Shadi's zip cuts through the stream of words.

"I need to go now," she says, getting to her feet.

"Great, well, thanks for coming," says Thorsten, with a slightly confused look on his face. Anna just lifts her hand in farewell.

"*Eternal Sunshine of the Spotless Mind!*" she exclaims triumphantly as Shadi closes the door behind her. As soon as she's in the hall, she takes out her phone. Luckily Emil picks up straight away.

"What's up, sweetheart?"

He sounds happy. Why can't she be too? Why does she always have to make things difficult? Sometimes it's like all she does is drag them both down.

"I finished the meeting," she says.

"Yeah, how did it go? You put that Anna girl in her place?"

But Shadi can't answer; her throat has seized up. It feels exactly like the time she caught her ring finger in a door and Amanda's mom drove her to the hospital with the tip in a bag of ice. She made it all the way into the operating room without crying, and everybody praised her for being such a big, brave girl. But the tears came the second her mother stormed through the door.

ANNA

BILLIE EILISH FOLLOWS ANNA AROUND as she flings clothes onto the bed, whirls through the living room, and ends up in the bathroom. The supervision this morning went surprisingly well, despite Shadi keeping her foot jammed on the brake. Now she's off to meet Siri.

As always, she takes the most time over the stuff underneath. Wash, shave, underwear. The rest varies. She'll wear makeup or not, do her hair this way or that. She fusses over her outfit for ages, trying on different combinations in front of the mirror, but in the end, she opts for the orange jumpsuit, eyeliner, and big earrings. There. She eyes herself appraisingly in the mirror, stroking her hair to one side. That'll have to do, she decides, and grabs her fake fur off the hanger. She's already late.

Before taking the three steps down into Caparnaum, she checks the time. Quarter past. It could have been much worse. Inside, in the warm, she undoes her top buttons. All around her there are couples and friends chatting away at small tables, while a bigger group clinks their beer glasses—and then, way over in the corner by the window, there she is. There's a jolt in Anna's chest when they make eye contact.

"So, making me wait on a first date, huh?" Siri gets up and holds out a long-fingered hand. It's soft against Anna's, which as always is covered in scratches and callused skin from training.

"Sorry," says Anna, and she gives a laugh. "My brain does this thing where it calculates distance as the crow flies, so I'm always taken aback when I have to go around buildings and stuff."

Their knees brush under the table as they sit down.

"Nice to see you again," says Anna.

"Really? I wasn't sure what you thought about it." Siri smiles at her.

"No, I'm glad you texted. I was just busy the other day. What was the book you borrowed, by the way? It looked heavy."

"Just something about patent law. It's good to stay up to date."

Anna nods earnestly. "The linchpin of any book collection."

"Exactly," laughs Siri, running a hand through her thick hair. Her features are delicate, with a slightly crooked nose and the kind of cheekbones Anna has always found more beautiful than almost anything else.

"I am actually a lawyer though," she adds. "It's not just a fetish. And what about you, you're a student?"

"Psychology." Anna nods. "All I've got left now is the dissertation. It's been a bit of a slow start because I took my time finding a supervisor."

Siri's smile is now so subtle that it's mostly just a special light in her eyes. "I sense a pattern emerging," she remarks, and Anna feels a rush of heat.

"All right, so maybe I can be a bit slow out of the gate. But after that, I'm all in," she says.

Again, knee grazes against knee, and instead of pulling away Anna leans further, pressing her thigh against Siri's. She wants to reach over the table and draw her in, but Siri is already moving closer, slowly, until their faces are barely an inch apart. Then she turns her head, gliding so close past Anna's cheek that she can feel her skin against her own, and whispers, "I want you."

Later, after Siri has put her clothes back on, kissed her goodbye, and disappeared into the Aarhus night, Anna lies awake for a while with the duvet thrown aside, cooling off. Her nipples are throbbing; her body feels light and supple, as though sex with Siri has knocked loose something in her she didn't know was stuck. She already wants her again. She feels a stupid urge to stay lying there amid the traces of their scents and the feeling of being touched everywhere and just wait for Siri to come back so they can start all over again. She sighs. Of *course* the one time somebody decides to leave is the one time Anna wishes she had stayed.

February 2012

ELISABETH

"THANK YOU," SAID ELISABETH, ACCEPTING the bouquet.

She stepped aside to let Malene and her family in. The children hugged her legs before scampering into the living room, but their bright voices were like knives, and for a moment she thought she'd have to send all four back home. That she wasn't ready yet to have small children in the house, to inhale their special scent and hold their unsteady weight as they climbed onto her lap and put their sticky hands in hers. Then, shaking it off, she went to get a vase. Since the funeral, she'd developed an aversion to severed stems and the taut-tied heads of flowers, and the aroma, especially of lilies, was now inextricably associated with the thought of death. But she set the bouquet in the middle of the dining table anyway.

"Please can we go up to Winter's room?" asked Amalie, suddenly standing in front of her. The mark above her eye had grown; it bulged, brown and pitted. Why didn't they just get it removed? Before Elisabeth could answer, Malene put an arm around her daughter.

"Why don't you stay down here with the rest of us, sweetheart? We've got our own toys to play with, haven't we?"

But the children nagged. They didn't understand why they weren't allowed to go upstairs and play with Winter's things the way they usually did. Later on, while Elisabeth passed around the tart and salads she'd spent hours preparing but now had lost any desire to eat, Mark told them about some windmills that would have to be demolished because they didn't comply with Brazilian regulations. And as Malene cut up food for August, Amalie slipped away from the table. Not to go to the bathroom, as they thought, but to climb the stairs. To steal along the corridor and over creaking boards to a door that wasn't meant to be opened.

"Why is it locked?"

Her shriek reverberated through the house. August began to cry, and Elisabeth sat amid the stench of the flowers, wishing the visit would be over soon. The children were right, this was all wrong. Winter was gone, his things had vanished, and his mother had become somebody else.

"I want to go into Winter's room," yelled Amalie again. The cry seemed to grow huge as it came down the stairwell.

"Sweet pea, why don't you come downstairs?"

Malene, who had picked up the sobbing August, smiled apologetically at Elisabeth. *We know how children are*, said her face, but Elisabeth could hear Amalie tugging at the door handle. She flew up the stairs, and as she reached the landing, she caught sight of the little girl. She had both hands on the handle, and at the sight of Elisabeth she flung herself against the door with all her might.

"I want to go in!" she shouted, and in her mind's eye Elisabeth saw the bawling, living child burst into Winter's room and pull everything apart. In two long strides she had reached Amalie, and she couldn't catch herself before the slap fell.

They were all in hats and coats when she came back down to the front hall. Mark couldn't even meet her eye. He muttered something and hurried off down the garden path with August in his arms. Malene stood holding on to Amalie, the red cheek like an accusation between them.

"She misses her friend. We all miss him, Elisabeth, and I do understand that this is hard for you. But this." Malene shook her head. There was something definitive in her expression.

After they had gone, Elisabeth went back into the front room. The table looked like some hysterical still life—half-eaten food, cutlery dropped mid-raise. And the wine, they'd emptied nearly two bottles. How much had she drunk?

Something swelled inside her as she stood there looking; she reached out for the bunch of flowers and yanked it, toppling the vase and one of the glasses. In the middle of it all was a strange satisfaction at the stalks' brittle snap when she broke them in half.

CHAPTER FIVE

September 2024

———

THORSTEN

"BEFORE WE GET STARTED," KAMILLA began, "I'd like to share some pretty interesting news that Elisabeth mentioned last time we spoke. It looks like Callocain won't only be released on the European market—apparently there's an American deal in the pipeline as well. What I'm saying is this is going to be big, okay, and that means our project will come under much greater scrutiny than we expected, both in Denmark and among our colleagues overseas. We at AU are on the cutting edge here, and I think we can be very proud of the work we've done!"

There's elation in the conference room. Cecilie is on the verge of breaking into applause. Thorsten doesn't quite know what to think; if they end up as leaders in the field of grief research, if they're the ones everybody else is obliged to cite, then that's fantastic news. On the other hand, he'd like to be completely sure they've got all their ducks in a row before they start to celebrate. So, while the others discuss the grief disorder conference they're going to host in the new year, he reserves judgment. It's not until Kamilla asks if there's anything else they need to discuss that he speaks up.

"There is one thing that surprises me about your results, Anton," he says, catching the statistician's eye. "Something that seems to me to be a mistake. Obviously, that makes me a little concerned we might be jumping the gun here."

Anton looks at him expectantly, his thin face unreadable. Thorsten continues.

"It's about a young man by the name of Mikkel Jespersen. He's undergone a significant drop in empathy over the course of the project, which is interesting in and of itself, of course. It's not something we've discussed properly yet, I think—how the empathy scores of the patients who received Callocain have failed to normalize. Why did we see this dramatic fall in certain cases? Why are many of them still scoring so unnaturally low, even though they're feeling better? And how do we reconcile this with our other results?" He lets the questions hang in the air for a moment. "But the mistake I'm talking about is that Mikkel scored five points in the most recent round of tests. Yet in your report, Anton, it says that the distribution of empathy scores across the entire sample was between seven and twenty-eight. So can you tell me what happened to Mikkel's score?"

"Anton?" Kamilla turns to him. There's silence in the room; no one moves.

"That must be an outlier." Anton's watery grey eyes meet Thorsten's.

"A what?"

"An outlier. A data point that differs so significantly from the others that it skews the overall result if it's included in the analysis. You can choose to leave those out."

"So you removed Mikkel's score because it's too extreme?"

Anton nods.

"And were there any others you picked out?" asks Thorsten. "Because if the results are so extreme, then it's not exactly—"

But that's as far as he gets before Kamilla interrupts.

"Great," she says, clapping her hands. "That explains that, then." She smiles at him. "Was there anything else?"

"There was, actually," he says, turning to Anton. "I just hope you're going to double-check that your analysis is accurate."

It's hard to interpret the statistician's grimace. Is it irritation making the corners of his mouth curl like that? He ought to be at least as keen as Thorsten is to make sure they don't flub this, but maybe he just doesn't like his professionalism being called into question.

"We know that people who are grieving can be weakened in several areas." Thorsten glances around the table. Most of his colleagues are listening closely, and although Svend looks like his mind has drifted, Thorsten knows he's paying attention. "Including the theory of mind and related functions, which we've chosen to call empathy. We've replicated that finding—so far, so good. But as I said earlier, we see an additional dip in empathy among those who have received the medication, even though from a purely grief-focused perspective they're feeling better." He taps the graph in front of him. "My common sense tells me their interest in other people should be returning to normal as they learn to cope, but evidently that isn't the case. What do we take from that?"

Cecilie opens her mouth, but Anton beats her to it.

"I'll leave the psychological interpretations to you, but I would like to emphasize that the small drop we're looking at is within the acceptable bounds of statistical uncertainty. So, it's more correct to say that there has been no change in the empathy score over time in any of the groups than that it has fallen in those who were given Callocain."

"Okay," says Thorsten, "but still. Why hasn't empathy gone up, as one might expect? Why is it still lower than in the general population?"

Cecilie leans forward. "Could we be looking at a delayed response? The experience of feeling better comes first, while other things, like empathy, catch up later on?" she suggests. "I wonder if they might have normalized if we tested them again in six months?"

"It's worth noting in our publications as a potential avenue for future research," Miguel says, nodding. "One of the theories about reduced empathy among people who are severely affected by grief is that they simply have less bandwidth available—for themselves as well as for others—and maybe that's still the case even after they've started feeling better. Not to mention that hell is other people, as we know—" he winks at Svend "—and if you allow yourself to love again, you make yourself vulnerable to the same thing happening twice."

Thorsten grunts. Their reasoning does fit with Louise's observations about Mikkel being unable to maintain close contact with his family after his loss. Anyway, Thorsten knows from his own experience that for many people it's a natural defence mechanism to close themselves off during that initial period.

To his immense surprise, Natasha, Rikke's timid PhD student, puts up her hand. Blotches of scarlet are creeping up over the collar of her shirt like climbing plants, and Thorsten gives her what he hopes is an encouraging smile.

"It could also be the medication," she says.

"A side effect, you mean?"

The question comes from Miguel, and Natasha nods, clearly relieved to be understood.

"Your explanations are psychological," she elaborates, "but if Callocain affects the brain, as we've seen from the scans, such that the memories of the deceased provoke a reduced emotional response compared to the control group, then could it be that the medication also suppresses empathy? I mean, it would be odd, wouldn't it, if Callocain worked so specifically that it *only* created emotional distance from the deceased?"

"Bang on!" Thorsten has never heard Natasha say so many words before. "I've been thinking exactly the same thing."

"Don't you think Danish Pharma would have noticed if Callocain had the kind of pronounced side effect you're talking about?" says Kamilla. "Let's be fair here. They've spent many more years and poured god knows how much more money into this than we have."

Natasha's eyes drop to the table. She seems almost to shrivel in her chair, and Thorsten knows she won't say anything else now.

"But they haven't studied empathy like we have," he objects. "It's a niche area—they're not set up for that kind of psychological testing. Anyway, there's something else. If I think about a person like Mikkel, who on paper has experienced a dip in empathy, well, that's not something he's complained about. Surely it's conceivable that this hasn't been reported as a side effect simply because people don't think it's a problem?"

"All right, then isn't the question whether it actually *is* the problem you're making it out to be?" Kamilla glances at her phone. "It's getting on. We need to table the rest of this discussion. I'll be calling most of you to another meeting in a month's time, but otherwise we'll be doing this via email from now on. The results are watertight?" She gestures toward Anton with the handout, her expression questioning, and he nods. "Right, then our next step is to make sure they're interpreted and presented in the best way possible. There'll be time for these more tangential discussions further down the road. I'll be issuing a press release on our provisional findings in the near future. Thanks for today."

Thorsten remains seated as the room empties around him. He still hasn't heard from Mikkel, but the least he can do is make sure the young man's test results have been handled properly. And if the others aren't interested in taking a closer look, well then, he'll have to do it himself.

SHADI

FIRST SHADI TAKES OUT THE easy things: black pants, under-wear, socks. She puts them on the chair, ready for tomorrow. She's supposed to count three tops onto the pile and take the fourth, but every once in a while there's a hiccup. Even when she takes the right top, it feels wrong, and she has to put it back and start from scratch, or else the whole system gets messed up. Then she can't decide if she should take it from the beginning or count from the place she's got to in the pile, and the heat starts spreading from her chest, rising like the tide toward her throat.

"You nearly finished, love?"

She's been standing in front of the wardrobe so long she thought Emil had fallen asleep. Her hands are trembling, she's desperate to let go, but she doesn't make the rules; she just struggles to follow them, and right now she's failing. "I don't know..."

Emil props himself up on his elbow. She hasn't told him about the clothes thing before, but he knows her well enough to see the quicksand when it's dragging her down. Then he's standing beside her, very calm, putting an arm around her shoulders.

"Which one are you thinking?" he asks.

Her voice is thick as she answers, "This one, maybe? Or that?"

She shows him the purple one, which was fourth in the pile first time round, then the white one she pulled out at the next count. It's impossible to choose now; nothing feels good.

"Hmm." Emil looks thoughtful. Her eyes are fixed on his face. "I've always liked the white one."

"Are you sure?"

Taking the top out of her hands, he gives her a hug. "Certain."

The sheet is cool against her skin as they climb into bed under the covers. Emil's breathing rapidly grows deeper, while Shadi lies there in the dark, doubt fluttering beneath her ribs.

The next day she stays home again, although Anna's texted to ask if they can get together soon to write. By now the dissertation is twenty pages long, and although it's just an outline, she's pleased with it. So far, she's been the only one adding to the folder, so when she sees something has appeared from Anna, she opens the document immediately. Time to see what all the fuss is about. But it makes no sense. The text she's looking at is so clumsily written that she wonders whether Anna might be dyslexic.

If she's put a comma, it's in the wrong place, several passages are missing words, and there are random spelling mistakes that could have been corrected with a single click. It looks like it's been written by a lunatic or a whirlwind. Or—wait. Once Shadi starts to read it properly, after her first superficial judgment, the obvious flaws begin to recede into the background. These aren't fragments culled from books and articles, paraphrased line by line and bundled up with references, and unlike in Shadi's section of the document, there are no copied-and-pasted blocks of text waiting to be slotted into place. What Anna has written is more like free-flowing thought. It's clear the words and opinions are her own, and although her claims are occasionally supported with academic citations or a remark in parentheses about having to find one, the pages have a character and tone Shadi would almost call literary. She didn't even realize you could write like that, and definitely not in a university paper.

A familiar weight in her belly disrupts her train of thought. Over the past couple of months she's noticed a change when her periods are due. Not something she's put into words yet, but it's different from when the blood was just a regular intrusion that vanished down the toilet bowl along with wads of paper. Emil can never understand where it all goes.

"Nobody has ever used as much toilet paper as you do," he exclaimed a few weeks after they'd moved in together. "I don't get what you do with it all."

She could have just told him. Explained how she places sheets of it over the seat when she thinks it might be dirty. How she uses the paper as a protective membrane between fingers and surface, for instance when she flushes, and again a moment later as she turns on the tap while her hands are still soiled; how many times she has to wipe before it feels okay. But she said nothing, trying to look mysterious, as though it were some special female riddle instead of an obsessive, insistent need.

And now this new sensation. She parts her thighs a little to watch the bloody thread as it detaches, turning to clouded water-colour in the bowl. No longer is it dross to be discarded but possibility, wasted month after month—a possibility she has neither the desire nor the courage to explore.

ANNA

IT'S BEEN FOUR DAYS SINCE Anna last heard from Siri. She hasn't texted either, of course, but for some reason it feels important that Siri is the one to get in touch. Desire has become a faint whine in her ears, making her scroll through long lists of Siris on Facebook, until it dawns on her she doesn't even know her last name. Instead, she checks her Hinge profile and stares at the two pictures Siri has uploaded. The one with the bun and the earnest, almost severe expression she could have taken herself. The other is older and taken from further away. Siri is in profile, sitting on a terrace and gazing down into a luxuriant garden. The wind is blowing her dark curls into her face, partially obscuring it, but the impression you get is different somehow from the first image. This was taken while something in Siri stood open, and Anna can't help but think she's looking at someone she loves. One day, thinks Anna, putting the phone back down, she will ask her who it is.

She's surprised by how much she wants to see Siri again, but her guard is probably further down now than it usually is. It's been a tough year. First there was the part when her mom got really sick—hectic and drawn-out and fear-filled. Then there was the part that came next, and she doesn't really know how to describe that, because she's still in it. Maybe it's getting better. She isn't crying as much these days. But it's also getting worse. Something inside her is rattling around, homeless, and every now and then she's scared it won't fall back into place.

By the time she opens her laptop, half the day has already somehow slipped through her fingers. That's why she's trying to get Shadi to spend a day writing together, but she's cold as ice. If she wants to know what she's working on, Shadi replied yesterday, Anna can just look in the shared folder. Great, thanks. Clearly all that matters to Shadi is avoiding actually having to talk.

Anna opens the document she's using for the dissertation and presses the spacebar a couple of times. Shadi has suggested she write a summary of the various approaches in the literature on grief up until the present day, but that's too boring. Her concentration blinks and switches off if she isn't utterly absorbed in what she's working on. Her brain works best in brief, intense spurts. So instead, she opens the browser. What she needs is a reality check. Danish Pharma has eclipsed every other medical company in the entire world with this new pill, which they must have started developing long before the diagnosis was even approved. Nobody else has been that quick, and from what Thorsten said it sounds like they'll be the undisputed top pharmaceutical dog in the field of grief therapy when Callocain hits the market. They must have something interesting to say.

She quickly looks up their website and shoots off an email saying who she is and how helpful it would be if she could come by for a chat. That done, she shuts the laptop again. That'll have to be enough for today. A couple of minutes later she's heading down the stairs with her gym bag bumping against her back.

April 2012

——

ELISABETH

IN THE BEGINNING ELISABETH KEPT her new project strictly
under wraps. A cure for grief. Not like the psychologists saw it,
oscillating in and out of the dark, or the priest with his assurances
of the blessings of the afterlife, but a cure her way, a chemist's way.
Her plan was to find the precise combination of drugs to rebalance
a grieving brain, but although it felt right, she didn't dare say it out
loud. Not yet.

Then the day came when, for the first time, she could see the
contours of its fundamental chemical structure. She spent most of
that night preparing and laid out her vision to her colleagues at
Danish Pharma, and although there were more than a few doubt-
ers, she was convincing enough that they agreed to try. Of course,
there were no guarantees that she would ever have a finished product. The very premise that grief could be mapped as a series of
neural changes and treated with medication was, to put it mildly,
bold. But there was hope, and the work kept her afloat. She set an
alarm and got to the lab before the night relaxed its grip, channel-
ling all her mental energies in one direction.

It had been one year since Winter died. Still, the knowledge
of it struck out of the blue. Sometimes it was the sound of a child
laughing, or the act of putting the key in the lock as she came
home, sensing in her body his presence right behind her, about to
run inside. She'd redecorated top to bottom, but there were land-
mines everywhere. Things she had to avoid thinking about, because
they dragged something dense and glutinous in their wake, places
she couldn't be. Then there were the special days, which had been
turned wrong-side out. Winter's birthday, Easter, Halloween. She'd
spent the first Christmas at Malene's, but that turned out to be
even worse than being alone, and in the middle of dancing around
the Christmas tree she'd had to run to the toilet to throw up. This

year she'd find an excuse to stay home, assuming Malene was even planning to invite her.

And so the time passed, without anything really getting better. The only bright spot was her new brainchild, growing bigger and stronger every day. The pill that was going to revolutionize the treatment of grief and make it possible to help others like her. The ones who didn't get better by talking about all the things they had lost.

CHAPTER SIX

September 2024

———

THORSTEN

"THORSTEN, HAVE YOU GOT TEN minutes?"

Kamilla keeps marching down the hall toward her office without waiting for an answer, and Thorsten follows with a deep sense of foreboding that he's about to be told off.

"So, Thorsten." Kamilla settles into her chair, gesturing toward the seat he's supposed to take. "First I'd like to know how you're getting on these days."

"I'm sorry?"

"Several of us have been thinking you've seemed a bit burned out lately. We're worried about you." Kamilla smiles. Is it him, or do her teeth seem a shade whiter than normal? Thorsten squints. Do they usually shine like that? "And I personally wasn't very impressed with the way you accused Anton of making a mistake the other day."

"No," says Thorsten, "but it was worth pointing out that Mikkel's score wasn't included. Even competent people can miscalculate."

"They can indeed." A sharpness has crept into Kamilla's voice. "But you've been working here for ages, Thorsten, and you know very well how it affects the group when you accuse someone of screwing up like that."

"To be honest, actually, I think it's a funny kind of research group that doesn't allow people to draw attention to potential mistakes," Thorsten protests, but Kamilla tuts in disapproval.

"It's the *way* you did it, Thorsten. Certainly I'm delighted to have you on board, and I appreciate you always wanting to push things that little bit further. But I'm afraid I feel you've got too involved in this project without me realizing, which is why I've just grabbed you. For the group's sake and for yours." What is she actually saying? And who has she been talking to behind his back?

"So I'm supposed to keep my mouth shut and fall into line?" he asks. "Is that it?"

Kamilla shakes her head, still smiling. If she were a cat she'd be purring, and Thorsten has never been fond of cats.

"What I'm saying is that if you needed a couple of days off I'd be more than happy to oblige. I know you've been through some rough patches."

"Are you seriously bringing up the one time I took compassionate leave fourteen years ago, Kamilla?" he bursts out. This is absurd. He and Kamilla didn't even know each other back then, when Anita walked out and he was sent home to lick his wounds for a few weeks, very much against his will.

"No, Thorsten, I'm not. I'm talking about the unfortunate episode with Rikke last year and your baseless accusations against her and her students—"

"Baseless? If I'd had even a smidgen of support from management we might actually have got to the bottom of that," protests Thorsten, but Kamilla carries on unperturbed.

"And the way you ran yourself into the ground, to the point where I wasn't sure whether to fire you or force you to take some time off. Is that ringing any bells?"

He's fidgeting on the hard seat, trying to find a more comfortable position. Kamilla is making him feel unpleasant, as though he's been stabbed in the back, but maybe she's right that things last summer got a little out of hand. He'd been convinced—still is, for that matter—that their post-doc Rikke had helped several of her students get artificially inflated grades in their written exams, and perhaps he had been a little insistent with his accusations. But he'd had no idea Kamilla actually considered letting him go.

"All I'm asking is that you come to me if you need anything, or if you have any other clarificatory questions about the project. That's much better than you burying yourself in all sorts of unnecessary—" she searches for the right word "—work."

He reaches out for the glass she's put out for him but misjudges the distance and sends water sloshing over the shiny wooden desk. Something about this conversation has rattled him.

"Now that you mention it, I do think we should take another look at our results, maybe get a second opinion," he says, in an attempt to regain some control over the situation, but Kamilla's eyes linger on him, making his movements awkward as he tries ham-fistedly to mop up the spilled water with his shirt sleeve. "I'd like a sensible answer as to why some of the patients' scores have been filtered out. I was one of the people involved in testing Mikkel, and I have no reason to believe his scores aren't valid. On the contrary, it's critical we find out why his and no doubt other participants' empathy scores dropped like that. Especially before we announce everything to the press, surely?"

"Thorsten." Kamilla's hands are now flat on her thighs. "You've established that one of your test subjects scored lower on the empathy questionnaire. So far, I'm with you. But now you're imagining that this says something about the project more generally? Or about Callocain, is that right?"

He hesitates. Should he tell her about the conversation with Louise, and the vague sense he has that they might be overlooking something crucial, something that goes far beyond Mikkel's results? No. Although he can usually trust his intuition, he still doesn't have enough to persuade Kamilla. It's better to continue the investigation on his own and wait until he has something more concrete to show for it.

"An isolated case or two," Kamilla adds, confirming him in that decision. "That doesn't prove anything, you know that. Remember the HPV scandal?"

Of course he does. The case had strained people's faith in experts and been a hot topic at the institute.

"The girls and their families were convinced the symptoms were caused by the vaccine. It got blamed for all manner of ills, even though the evidence showed that side effects were minimal and the complaints could be explained in other ways. People refused to listen. They had their own opinions, and they were utterly impervious to fact. If the research showed there was nothing wrong with the vaccine, then the researchers were corrupt, bought and paid off by Big Pharma. And if you ignored the broader picture and only listened to one-off stories—the elite gymnast who had the world at her feet until she got the shot, or whatever—it was easy to get dragged along by the bandwagon. These days, however, we don't conduct research based on gut instinct and isolated cases."

Kamilla's smile is almost eerily gentle now. "We gather the data and process the statistics methodically. And since none of your colleagues have expressed the same reservations, Thorsten, I'm going to be frank with you. I think you need to let this go. Stop looking for something that isn't there, and let us bring this project to a proper, dignified conclusion. Do we understand each other?"

But before he's even back in his own comfy armchair, Thorsten is planning his next move. Kamilla's feigned concern and barely concealed directive to back off and mind his own business has only made him more determined to figure out what's going on. It's more than a matter of professional integrity now—he's not going to let some efficiency-obsessed bureaucrat get away with wagging an overbearing finger at Thorsten Gjeldsted.

SHADI

"EXCUSE ME?"

Shadi knocks cautiously. Thorsten is at his desk, which as usual is a jumble of books, stacks of articles, and loose sheets of paper.

"Shadi?" His first confused expression morphs into a smile. "What can I do for you?"

Relieved that he seems pleased to see her, she forces out the sentence she's been turning over in her head for days and practised all the way from the reading room. Even so, she stumbles over the words.

"It was just…you said at some point there might be something in your grief project we could use for the dissertation?" In the pause that follows, she has time to regret she even asked. Then Thorsten's face brightens.

"Oh, of course, that's quite right. It's actually in among all this stuff." He nods at the clutter in front of him. "We've just had the first report come in on the results, and although there are a few points we need to clarify, I don't think there's any reason why you can't read it too. If you're lucky, we'll have an article or two under review before you submit. So you can be the first people in the world to cite us."

"Great," says Shadi, although she has no idea what kind of review he's talking about. "We'd love to."

"I've already sent some of the background material to Anna," says Thorsten. "There's some information on diagnosis and standard treatment that might serve as inspiration."

Shadi doesn't understand why he's sent something to Anna without also sending it to her, but she says nothing. What matters is to make Thorsten see that she's at least as talented and ten times as hard-working as his former favourite pupil.

At his prompting she starts to spell her email address, which he jabs laboriously into his computer with a single pointed index finger and a worryingly long hunt for the at-sign. Because he's emailed her before, the address autofills, but Thorsten doesn't notice.

"Right," he says when he's finished. "As you know, Danish Pharma are planning to launch Callocain onto the domestic market very soon, and they've had some excellent results from their own trials, which we've tried to replicate, of course. But the real goal of our project is to test various hypotheses about how Callocain works. Not biochemically but cognitively, personality-wise, and so on."

"I've read a bit about it," Shadi interjects. That's an understatement. She's looked up the project on the university's website several times, and she read all the information she could get her hands on when she chose the topic of her dissertation.

"That's great," says Thorsten. "Then just take a look at what I've sent and pipe up if you have any questions. But don't rely too heavily on the results yet, because they are still subject to change."

"I thought the project was finished." Shadi doesn't want to sound stupid, but she doesn't get how the results can change if the trial is over.

"That may well be so. There are just a few details I can't quite…" Thorsten's gaze wanders back to the papers on his desk, and when he starts speaking again it's as though he's no longer talking to Shadi. "I know I'm not the one doing the analyses, so maybe I should stop poking my oar in, but I really can't accept any mistakes here. This project is simply too important."

He sighs and removes his glasses, rubbing his already pink eyes. When he turns his face back to Shadi, he looks like someone waking from a long sleep.

"Can't you just check the calculations yourself, if you're not sure?" she asks cautiously, but he only looks more at sea.

"Well, that's what I'm trying to do, but I've never been on a particularly friendly footing with these statistical programs," he confesses. "They didn't exist when I was training, and ever since I've been here, I've been lucky enough to have people to do it for me."

She should probably leave it there, but she knows only too well the urge to erase that gnawing doubt before it gets its teeth in properly. "I could take a look at it for you," she suggests carefully. "If you like."

"Could you?" Thorsten's eyes widen. "Are you good with that sort of thing?"

"Yeah," she replies. It's hardly that surprising. "I mean, we did stats in third year, but that was pretty surface-level, so I ended up buying the program myself."

"Goodness." Thorsten surveys her thoughtfully, but just as she thinks he's about to say yes, he shakes his head. "No, I can't have my students doing my research for me. But thank you, it's kind of you to offer."

Afterwards, heading down the path toward the library, she kicks herself for even asking. They finally have a conversation where she doesn't come across as a complete idiot, and then she has to take it too far. Obviously Thorsten doesn't need help from a student when he's got an entire research group at his disposal. What was she thinking? Emil will probably say it's good that she took some initiative, but all she can think is how frustrating it is to stick her neck out for once, only to be rejected.

ANNA

"HI, DAD."

He opens the door and stands there with his glum smile, which pushes up his cheeks but doesn't reach his eyes. His sloppy shave scratches Anna's cheek. She steps out of her shoes and hangs up her jacket while he just lingers, leaving her to enter the kitchen first. The place mostly looks the way it has ever since she was little, but there's a different feeling to it now. A stranger wouldn't be able to put their finger on it, but it feels as though nothing new, neither oxygen nor object nor person, has crossed the threshold for a very long time, and she's seized by a powerful urge to grab her father's hand and save him from it.

"Let me know if there's anything you need." He looks rather helplessly around him, gesturing toward the living room. "I've tried to gather up some of Mom's things, but I haven't got that far with it, I guess."

She knows she should offer to help, but right now she doesn't have it in her. "It'll get done," she says. "Don't stress about it."

The meal is awful. The potato wedges and greyish steaks her dad eats come straight from the freezer, the salad is one of the ready-made ones from the supermarket, and she suppresses the impulse to tear a strip off him for taking such bad care of himself. Instead, she talks about literally anything else.

"It's going to be a critical analysis of the new grief diagnosis," she says. "This isn't the first time in history that people have been called sick as a way of gaining power over them, you know."

As always when she talks about her studies, she makes an effort to choose words her father will understand. Not because he's stupid, far from it, but because when she started university after a lucky second-round application, she was taken aback by the amount of new terminology. She could feel herself storing up terms like *discourse* and *performative utterances,* questioning old truisms and slowly changing both her thinking and her language. Several times she's had the feeling that in her parents' eyes she's started to seem downright hoity-toity. Neither of them really understood why she stopped eating meat, and conversations about politics and social justice gradually became so inflammatory that she's got used to skirting around them.

Eventually she stops speaking. Her father's jaws are grinding back and forth; he never quite swallows everything before he shovels in a new wedge. The sound of food being macerated and softened and wetted anew, the glass greasy as he washes it down.

"So you're writing about grief?" he says at last. "I suppose that's one way of dealing with things." He pushes the knife so that it lies parallel with the fork.

"It's not some weird form of self-therapy, if that's what you mean," she says, instantly regretting how harsh she sounds. "I mean, it doesn't have anything to do with Mom."

"If you say so." He looks up. "Have you been to the cemetery recently?"

Anna shakes her head. She thought she might have got away with not discussing it, but apparently here all roads lead to Mom. "It makes me claustrophobic."

"Claustrophobic?"

"I hate cemeteries. Anyway, I don't need to be in a specific place to remember her."

Her dad smiles—a small, thin smile. "No, she's with us everywhere, a bit too much perhaps. Could be. But I've started writing a list each night of things I can do—tidying one of the cupboards, for example, or putting some of her clothes in a garbage bag. It was my doctor's idea."

Anna jerks to her feet. She needs to get away from the table, and all these little steps that don't lead anywhere. Can't he hear himself? "You told me that, Dad."

He lowers his head over his food, and she feels like shit. The dishwasher door slams into its hinges, and her plate lands beside all the other lone plates that have been slotted in one at a time after yet another dinner in front of the TV. Like stomping on a wounded animal.

SHADI

"WHAT ARE YOU DOING, SHADI joon?"

Her mother's voice is light. Something's playing in the background, probably the radio in the kitchen, and Shadi can see her in her mind's eye. Phone wedged between her ear and her shoulder while her hands fly, smartening something, keeping it all going.

"Not much. I just finished writing for today."

"And Emil?"

"Still at work."

Shadi knows what's coming next. Her parents love Emil, but they never miss a chance.

"It's lovely that he's ambitious, but he works too much, your Emil. It's not good for the heart."

Her mother's reiterative song, a rolling flood of anxiety that Shadi has listened to for as long as she can remember.

"And you sitting there with that essay all day long. Will they let you start again if it doesn't come out right?" She wants to know, and Shadi answers just as she did the last time she asked, that no, they won't.

"Only if I fail."

"Fail?" Her mother shoves away the word as though it were a fetid tea towel. "But then what will you do? Can you extend your studies, or maybe your grant won't last that long?" The torrent is coming faster now, whipping up stones and leaves from the riverbed. "You know you can always borrow money from us if you can't manage, my love."

"Mom, why are we even talking about this? I'm not going to fail."

"You were the one who said it!" Now she's brought out the injured tone she always uses when Shadi or her younger sister have been unfair. "But maybe it wouldn't be the worst thing, you know. I read somewhere that unemployment is sky-high for newly qualified psychologists. Most of them get their first job by networking. But you don't have a part-time job, Shadi joon, even though I told you about that doctor lady who needs an assistant."

Shadi scrunches up her eyes. She's got to remind herself that her mother means well. There's no reason to pick a fight over something that doesn't exist.

"How's it going with Bassu?" she asks, and it works. While her mother tells her about her aunt's bad back, she takes the phone away from her ear. Emil has texted. He's going for a few beers with someone from work, he says, followed by an irritating emoji and two tankards.

On a Thursday? she texts, and she wants to plead with him to come straight home, to make him promise it will only take an hour, two at most.

She watches the dots blinking on the screen.

People do occasionally go out and have fun on weekdays without it being the end of the world.

"Joon?"

Shadi stares at the phone. This is where she needs to drop it. To stop being the type of clingy girlfriend no one likes.

So when are you coming home? She hits Send before she can stop herself. No blinking dots, nothing but her own unsteady pulse. She clamps her hand against the top of her chest. He isn't going to answer.

"Shadi, can you hear me?"

"Yes!" she yells, putting the phone back to her ear. "But I've got to go now, Mom. Emil is here."

October 2013

——

ELISABETH

THE AFTERNOON ELISABETH'S TEAM AT Danish Pharma officially set its sights on a target, she was so exhausted it was hard to stay upright.

"We've got it!" they crowed to each other excitedly, and somebody produced a bottle of champagne. They had zeroed in on the dopaminergic receptors, and she was utterly convinced they had now found at least part of the neural correlate for complex grief. They had, in other words, a working theory of what went wrong in the brains of people who were mired in their grief, and everybody knew what that meant. They had made it through the first stage in one piece, and now the hunt began for the real purpose of all this. A cure.

"Go home and get some sleep, Elisabeth."

Sofia gave her arm a squeeze. She was one of the few people who hadn't reacted to the change Elisabeth had undergone since Winter's death. She was neither more distant nor less, but treated her just as before. Elisabeth returned her smile. Over the last year she had pushed herself harder than she ever would have done while Winter was alive. Often, she'd have food brought to the office in the evenings, and the neighbour's girl looked after Nala whenever Elisabeth chose work over home. The few hours she did sleep, she dreamed of complex molecule formations.

"Thank you for all your hard work," she said, raising her hand in a limp wave. "Great job, everybody!"

On the way home she drove as though through a heavy fog; she could hardly remember being so shattered. She woke twelve hours later just to call in and say she would be sleeping from home that day.

"Working," she corrected herself swiftly, but the secretary laughed and said it was well-deserved, and as she lay in bed an unfamiliar calm spread through her limbs. They were heading in the right direction.

CHAPTER SEVEN

September 2024

——

ANNA

SHE'S HITTING HOME. THE FRUSTRATION she has felt since visiting her dad and still not having heard from Siri has gathered in her muscles, a quivering tension, and by the time she's finished warming up she only wants to fight.

"Hey, Isam, you got anyone leftover?" she yells. He turns away from the gangly boy he's busy teaching.

"You can go a round with me in a minute, if you've got the balls."

She holds up a middle finger and keeps warm by drilling a few short combinations. Tightening her left glove, she resolves for the tenth time to be kinder when she next sees her dad. Plus, she's really got to help him tidy; it can't be good to let things pile up like that.

Finally, Isam is ready. They don't spar much, but there's no doubt who's better. He's both faster and stronger, and Anna's only real weapons in the skirmish are her kick and the fact that she isn't afraid. She isn't scared of pain—in fact, it's what she wants.

It will leave her exposed, but she strikes first anyway. He parries easily, and then she feels the singing thud of his fist against her cheekbone. He's hit her there to goad her, but there's no serious weight behind it. She feints left and counters with a kick, aiming for the kidneys, but Isam has seen her fight too many times. Deftly he grabs her foot, and a second later she's on the mat with the air hammered out of her lungs.

"So?" he pants, straddling her.

She lashes out, clipping his shoulder. "Just hit me," she hisses between her teeth. "Come on!"

There and then she wants nothing but to feel a bone snap inside, to feel her skin tear.

But instead he grabs her by the throat and squeezes. "I don't hit girls when they're down."

He grins crooked-toothed as she struggles to free herself, kicking uselessly and trying to twist him off her, but he's got a firm hold, and now he's applying so much pressure that it's cutting off her airway. She tries to hit him in the face, but he's keeping millimetres out of range, and although she claws and snatches at his arms to make him let go, he's too strong. For a few seconds more she thrashes in his grip. Then she gives up and shuts her eyes, though all her reflexes are screaming at her to act. This must be the ultimate control, she thinks, as her vision goes black. To lie quite still and accept death as it comes.

Then he lets go. A few quick slaps. "Hey, are you okay?"

She opens her eyes and gasps for air. "Idiot," she wheezes.

Isam winks. "That's what you wanted, isn't it?"

Then he gets up and wanders over to a group of girls who have just come out of the change room. Anna stays down as the whine fades. As much as her throat is sore, it feels as though her windpipe is expanding with each breath, even bigger now than it was before. Oxygen streams through. For the first time in days, the pressure behind her forehead is gone.

SHADI

IT'S FIVE THIRTY IN THE morning when Emil comes home, and Shadi knows something is very wrong. Neither of them says a word, but he lies down next to her still in his clothes and falls straight to sleep. He reeks of the pub. Shadi lies quietly, watching him in the pallid light. Remembering the day one year ago when it first struck her he might not be truly happy. She tried to talk to him about it, saying she was scared of losing him, that she couldn't cope without him. It had felt right, but she's wondered since if it was also a way of making him stay. *If you go, I'll fall apart.*

Not long after that they went for a walk in the woods and got lost, and Emil shouted that she could fucking figure it out herself. *Why is it always me that has to save us?* he had roared, and Shadi had begun to cry, because she didn't recognize his twisted face. Gingerly she sits up in bed. Strokes his hair.

"I slept with someone else," he says hoarsely.

And everything inside her drops. "Shadi?" Her head sinks toward her chest.

"Sorry, love." His voice is bleary with sleep or booze, and all she wants is for him to stop talking. "I'm just so sorry."

"Who was it?"

"Does it matter? You don't know her anyway."

He sits up beside her and starts apologizing again, but she doesn't want to hear it.

"No," she says. "Tell me who it is."

"Lucia," he mumbles. "Her name's Lucia. From work."

Has she heard that name before? Shouldn't she be able to remember it if her boyfriend had mentioned a woman by the name of Lucia from work, who he'd like to have sex with?

"Love?"

Emil's hand is hanging in the air between them, and Shadi can feel the pressure of his body, even though they're not touching. As though all of him is turned in her direction. But the hand never reaches her, and she's sitting quite alone, floating, untethered.

Maybe she genuinely can't live without him. *Touch me then*, she wants to say, *if it's me you want, then touch me.*

"I'm so sorry." Emil is crying now. "I wish it didn't happen, but it's just become so stifling here."

Stifling. He actually said stifling, and she feels like punching him. Her skin contracts around her; there's less and less space.

"What are you saying?" she asks.

"I didn't mean it like that, it's just…" There's something imploring about his tone now. He wants her to understand something, but it's hard to listen when she can't breathe. "I miss going out with my friends without feeling bad. I want—" He cuts himself off again. "We haven't even hit thirty yet, Shadi, but we live like we're in our fucking eighties!"

He must have thought about this a lot. The words are tumbling out of him now. Some of them she hears, others just slip past her. She can't cope with the effort anymore. It's been an effort too long, he's right, it's all so heavy. Something is pressing on her lungs. She wants to get up, but there's no air.

"Something's got to give, or this isn't going to end well," says Emil, but she doesn't understand what he means. It's already ended.

THORSTEN

THORSTEN WAKES OF HIS OWN volition before the alarm goes off. Today he's planned an alternative route to work. Only a minor detour, he tells himself over breakfast, a single impulsive twitch of the wheel. But the truth is that barely an hour later he's driving off in the opposite direction from the institute, out of the city toward Tilst, and if he'd bumped into a colleague on the way he would have been hard-pressed to explain what he was doing.

It's entirely possible that, as usual, he's on the brink of crossing a line. He's been accused on more than one occasion of being a little overdedicated. Of spending too much time on one student in whom he glimpses something bright, or going too far in an attempt to help an especially troublesome client. Anita had given him an entire mini-lecture about how the job took up ninety per cent of his energy while she and Andreas had to carve up the remaining ten between themselves; and although back then he'd thought she was being unfair, there was probably more truth to her words than he'd been willing to understand. The reality is simply that he doesn't know how else to live. If you don't let things matter, then what's the point? Why even be a psychologist if you aren't interested in the people at the heart of it all? So yes, he's taking a detour.

He's driving against the morning traffic, and after barely twenty minutes with jazz on the radio and the volume turned up to eleven, he's parking outside a detached pastel-yellow house. A white picket fence surrounds a strip of lawn that's both too narrow and too wilted to be called a garden. In one corner, squashed against the hedge beside the neighbouring plot, is a stroller. It appears to have been there for quite a while. The wheels are muddy, the hood askew as though someone's yanked at it, and something about the battered carriage makes Thorsten briefly want to turn and hurry back the way he came.

He stands a little irresolute, business card in hand. Further down the road a car door slams, but otherwise it's almost disconcertingly quiet. The grey sky is stretched across the city like a tight-fitting membrane; it might start raining at any moment. Then he pulls himself together and walks up to the front door. He can hear the bell ring inside, a loud, peevish trill. Nothing happens. He's about to stuff the card—on which he's written a note to say please get in touch—through the letterbox, but then his legs take a step to one side almost of their own accord, into the bushes outside the kitchen window. A combination of grime and glare means he has to lean forward, shadowing his eyes with his hand and pressing his face to the glass. And there—like a trick of the light—a male figure flits across the kitchen doorway. Is it him? Still in the same awkward position, Thorsten takes out his phone and dials the number he now knows by heart. As usual there's no answer, but there's the figure again, and before he can ask himself if it's the right thing to do, he's knocking on the pane.

"I'm so sorry to be hounding you like this," he says when Mikkel finally opens the door. It's good to see him again, not as a number in a list or a bluish brain in Anton's report but as a young man with bedhead, alive and kicking. "I just wanted to be completely sure you're doing okay before we let you go."

"Yeah, thanks." Mikkel conceals a yawn. "I'm fine."

Since he seems to have no intention of inviting him inside, Thorsten takes a step backward, away from the doormat. "I'm glad to hear that," he says. "You've been a hard man to get hold of. I think your sister misses you too, by the way."

"Louise?" Mikkel looks surprised. "I didn't realize. That's just life, isn't it? You're busy, so you drop the ball a bit with that stuff."

Thorsten nods, although he thinks it's a funny way to phrase it.

"She can't seem to get her head around it—I don't need to be constantly wallowing in all that. You know, about Julie and Thea." Mikkel pulls a face. "And after a while it just gets old, the guilt-tripping."

"No, of course. But apart from that, things are going well?"

"Yeah, I think so."

"And, um…" Thorsten hesitates. He thinks of Mikkel's empathy score in the last round of tests, but on the spot, he can't work out how best to ask. "What about the social side of things?"

"The social side?"

"Yes, I'm thinking of friends, that sort of thing. You've stopped coaching, I heard?"

Mikkel shrugs, stifling another yawn.

"But I suppose you've found another way to spend your time?" Thorsten persists, and a spasm of irritation crosses Mikkel's face.

"Like I said, I've got enough on my plate," he says, with a wave of his wrist. On it is a large sports watch, the kind that looks as though you could take it to the bottom of the ocean and it would still work.

"Of course." Thorsten gives him his most disarming smile. "There's just one more thing. I know you're feeling better, but could you try to explain to me what's changed? What's the biggest difference from when you first got involved with the project?"

For a moment Mikkel only looks at him wearily. Then he sighs. "It's a bit like seeing a film, you know? You remember the plot fine, and if a friend asks, you can tell them about it or say if you think it was good or bad. And that's what it's like." He gestures toward the stroller. "I know what happened, and I have no problem telling you how awful it was after the accident. It's just—it doesn't feel like the story is about me anymore."

ANNA

ANNA HOLDS OUT THE GLASS for a refill. She's lying with a pillow at her back and her legs around Siri. Siri, who abruptly called and asked if they were going to see each other again or what? Who almost ran up the stairs when she arrived, trailing the scent of an exclusive perfume and the evening air. Who is now sitting in Anna's boxy one-bedroom apartment, pouring expensive wine into her scratched old tumbler.

"It sounds like you're pretty fond of this Thorsten," she remarks, as Anna is in the middle of telling her about the dissertation.

"He's just really good," she says. She doesn't know Siri well enough to work out what she means, and her face betrays nothing. "He was my supervisor before, and we kind of stayed in touch. But don't go getting jealous." She prods Siri with her foot. "He's even older than you are!"

She laughs raucously, and Siri pushes the bottle further onto the coffee table.

"No more wine for the lady," she says, disentangling herself. "Do you have anything to eat around here?"

Anna shrugs. She doesn't actually know. Minutes later she can hear Siri opening and closing all the cupboards in the kitchen.

"Might be some biscuits in the corner cupboard," she shouts, and goes to pee.

Sitting on the cold seat, the tips of her toes pressed against the tiles, it's obvious she's drunk. How did that happen? Siri doesn't seem any the worse for wear, but then maybe she's one of those magical creatures who can knock back insane amounts of alcohol without getting plastered. Anna's best friend at school was like that. She'd be the one loyally walking Anna home after a pub crawl, a firm grip on her arm, the one who warmed up garlic bread in the oven and made her drink two big glasses of water before they keeled over intertwined and slept until they got so thirsty they woke up.

She can't hear Siri in the kitchen anymore. Maybe she's given up, or there really was a packet of biscuits somewhere. She quickly checks her phone. Shadi has finally agreed to meet up, but she didn't answer her last text, and the document in the shared folder, unusually, hasn't been touched since the day before yesterday.

"Did you find anything?" she asks as she walks back into the front room. Siri is standing by the desk where Anna's notes and articles are spread out, and she must have accidentally touched the keyboard, because the computer is glowing behind her.

"Just this."

She holds up a bag of dried apricots, and before Anna can ask what she was doing over there she's standing in front of her, putting her arms around her neck and kissing her so it tickles.

"Tell me something—" she plucks down the collar of Anna's turtleneck and brushes her fingers across her throat, where Isam's hands left greenish marks "—did somebody try to kill you?"

"You could put it like that. My trainer went a bit nuts. He said I needed it."

"Aha." The light is playing in Siri's eyes; her fingertips on the sensitive skin bring goosebumps out in Anna. "And was he right about that, you think?"

Anna smiles. She feels like Siri gets the urge she also has to push the world away. Like maybe she even feels the same. She's giddy as she leans in. "You taste good," she murmurs, with lips that are numb with wine. "Apricot kisses."

June 2015

ELISABETH

OVER SEVERAL MONTHS, ELISABETH HAD established a new
routine. Every day when she woke up, she poured herself a glass of
juice and swallowed one of the pills she had so adroitly made dis-
appear from the lab at Danish Pharma when nobody was looking.
For God's sake, she thought as she stuffed yet another stolen handful into her pocket, it was her own invention after all. The loss was
noted, as usual, but nobody suspected the drug might have been
taken by someone at the lab, and certainly not at such an early
stage. So far, Callocain—as she had decided to name her pills—
had been tested only on animals, and there was the obvious draw-
back that you couldn't ask them any questions. All they had to go
on were observations and measurements. Elisabeth, on the other
hand, was able to interrogate herself and note everything she felt
in the notebook beside the fridge, and although a single subject
was a hopelessly flimsy source of information, it was better than
nothing. Anyway, she needed close involvement.

Muscle cramps, dry mouth, bouts of drastic mood swings, and
bothersome heart palpitations that took months to go away. As
soon as she detected something out of the ordinary, it went into
the book, and she held review meetings with herself every Sunday
evening. Crossed out headache, added nausea. Considered whether
she had urinated more frequently than normal in the previous
week, or whether it was her imagination. And each time, as the
pen glided over the page, she thought: the grief is worse. None of
this comes anywhere close.

She had the lists at the back of her mind when she went into
Danish Pharma, and more than once her private experiment influ-
enced which way she decided to go. She and her unwitting colleagues polished and adjusted, scrutinized the animals in their
cages and the numbers on their screens, and as time went on the
list of side effects grew shorter. Not only that, but she thought she

was also beginning to feel the purpose of the whole thing. The relief. The way the pills subdued the respirator's muttering sea, which even now, years later, kept washing through her dreams. The way the chemical compounds that would one day be hailed as the world's first grief medication spun an ever-thicker web across the crater in her chest.

CHAPTER EIGHT

September 2024

———

THORSTEN

"RIKKE," CALLS THORSTEN, CATCHING SIGHT of her in the corridor outside, but she doesn't seem to hear him. Struggling out of his chair, he hurries after her.

"If you've got the time, I'd like to take a quick peek at your results from the EQ test," he puffs as he draws level with her. "Just to see if any of your test subjects scored below a seven."

Rikke is as tall as he is, which is to say around five foot ten, and takes incredibly long strides, making her an effort to keep pace with. The rebuff is plain on her face.

"I don't know what you're up to, Thorsten." She pauses outside her office. "But I do actually have other things to spend my time on, as I'm sure you can imagine, what with teaching and supervisions and the new project I'm starting up. So if you're still not sure about the figures or whatever, why don't you take a look at the database or take it up with Anton. The rest of us have moved on."

Of course. He should have guessed. Calling his relationship with Rikke tense would be an understatement, but he'd hoped they could let bygones be bygones, at least for a minute. It's ironic that he was the one to hire her, but his first impression had been good, and her CV very impressive. After a while, however, he thought he'd glimpsed a more calculating nature behind it. There was the discussion about research ethics he'd overheard at the Christmas party, when she got increasingly snide with every drink. This, he remembers thinking as she belittled one PhD student after another, isn't just a nasty side that comes out when she's tipsy. This is how she really is.

Then, of course, there was the whole blowup last summer, what Kamilla called Thorsten's baseless accusations. In his view, the matter should have been investigated a good deal more fully than it was. If he was correct that Rikke was helping her students cheat on the exam, she should have been thrown out on her ass. But there was no concrete proof, and the whole thing was quickly hushed up by Kamilla and the rest of the admin team. Since then, the air between Thorsten and Rikke has been distinctly icy, and now, he thinks as he watches her walk into her office and demonstratively shut the door, it's pretty damn inconvenient that the hatchet wasn't better buried.

Back in his chair, he logs into the shared drive. He doesn't use it much, but Rikke was right—after a bit of searching he finds the database that includes her results as well.

The quantity of numbers is overwhelming. He squints, using his finger to guide him down the flickering rows. There, a combined empathy score of six. He keeps going; several times he has to start again because he loses his thread. But then there it is in the middle of the spreadsheet—a four, even lower than Mikkel's. He leans back, exhausted. Three subjects whom Anton has chosen to leave out. He wonders what that means for the bigger picture.

There's chatter and footsteps in the corridor. It's nearly lunch-time, but when Svend pokes his head through the doorway Thorsten waves him on ahead.

"I'm coming," he says. "Just need to finish up here."

On the notepad, where he's jotted a three, he now puts a dash and writes: *big drop*. What he's doing here isn't exactly inspired sci-ence. But it bothers him that a young man like Mikkel, and maybe others like him, can have something as fundamental as empathy be affected without anybody asking why. Of course, he could take the view, like Kamilla, that the big picture is the only one that mat-ters, but the big picture only exists by virtue of all the little ones. Behind each of the numbers Thorsten is looking at is a rickety stroller abandoned in a front garden, an empty place at the din-ner table. Each drop in empathy has the potential to make a huge impact on people's lives.

He runs his finger across the screen, trying to compare the two columns: empathy when it was first tested, then again when it was tested six months later, for all the participants in the pro-ject. But the two aren't adjacent, and the numbers skip and jump before his eyes. Still, by the end of it he's left with eight exam-ples in his notepad, although he's far from sure he got them all. Eight people whose ability to empathize with others has nosedived so dramatically in the past six months that in Thorsten's opinion something is glaringly wrong. Eight people with a score under ten, setting off warning lights in Thorsten's brain. But then again, how is he supposed to decide whether eight out of 398 is a lot or a little? Whether his definition of a big drop is a reasonable one? Frustrated, he scratches at his neck.

The answer, of course, is that he can't. If he wants to figure out whether there's really any cause for concern here, then he's going to need some help.

SHADI

SOMETHING RIPS INTO THE DARK and drags Shadi out. She fumbles drowsily for her phone, but when she finds it, it's switched off. It takes a long time to grope her way through the fog; she doesn't know what time it is, only that she fell asleep at last after what felt like several days in a trembling, sped-up state. When it dawns on her that it's not the phone she can hear but the doorbell, her first thought is of Emil. That he's come home to tell her it was all a mistake, that he never should have left. But the second she turns on her phone, it starts to ring. It's Anna, and the jingle marries with the wearing chime of the bell. When the ringing finally stops, a text appears onscreen in capital letters: OPEN THE DOOR!

At last she gives in. Anna clearly has no intention of leaving. In the hall she catches sight of her face in the mirror. Skin grey-brown and dry, eyes oddly lifeless. She looks, in other words, exactly as she feels, and after opening the door a crack she goes into the bathroom to run cold water over her head.

"Hello? Shadi?"

The towel smells of Emil. She hesitates a moment, face buried. Then she tears herself away and goes into the hall.

"Hey," she says. The sound barely leaves her mouth.

"What's going on?" asks Anna. "I've been trying to get hold of you for days."

The apartment is dark, unlit but for the waning daylight, and to Shadi there's something revealing about it, as though anyone could see that something here has crumbled.

"What day is it?" she asks.

"Seriously?" Anna eyes her skeptically. "It's Tuesday."

Then she takes Shadi into the kitchen and sits her at the table before she sets about making coffee. She clearly knows exactly how to operate Emil's brute of a machine, and Shadi doesn't have the energy to tell her how much she loathes the taste. Grateful to no longer be alone, she lets Anna's small talk and the familiar sounds cocoon her like a woollen blanket, and when a mug is pressed into her hand she obediently takes a sip.

"Right, spit it out, then," says Anna. "What's happened? You stood me up yesterday, and now you look like you've been hit by a truck. Repeatedly."

Yesterday? At first, Shadi has no idea what Anna is talking about, but then she remembers. That in a past life, before the conversation with Emil, she'd agreed to meet up with Anna. Part of her is scared she'll make it true if she says it out loud, but that's just magical thinking, she knows that. Things are the way they are.

"It's my boyfriend, Emil. He slept with someone from work, and now he's gone to stay with his cousin."

Anna sucks the air between her teeth, as though something hurts. "How long were you together?"

"Nearly eight years."

Unhesitatingly Anna pulls Shadi into a kind of hug that catches her entirely by surprise. Her first impulse is to shrink away, but then she realizes it's not actually unpleasant. Just unfamiliar.

"It'll be okay," says Anna, letting go. "Either you'll dump him and find someone better or you'll work it out. Personally, there's no way I'd take someone back if they did that to me, but hey." She throws out her hands. "It's not like I've been with anybody longer than a year, so." She looks around. "Nice place, by the way."

"It belongs to my parents." Shadi swallows the tears creeping up her throat. "We talked about buying them out when I finish university, but now I don't know…"

Anna nods. She's found the milk in the fridge and starts to pour before Shadi realizes what she's doing.

"Stop!" she cries.

But it's too late. The clumpy white pulp swills out of the carton and into Anna's cup, and Shadi turns away in disgust.

"You've got yourself into a mess, haven't you?" Anna says. "Why don't I slip out and get some groceries? You look like you'd be better off staying in today."

And then the tears come after all.

"You don't have to do that," she protests, but Anna is already taking her jacket off the hook.

"Back in ten. Any requests? Otherwise it'll be a hundred per cent veggie, you know that!"

Shadi has only managed a superficial rinse of the sink, where the milk has congealed into a thick mousse around the drain, before Anna rings the bell again.

"Good, nourishing food is essential in a crisis," she says when she's stepped out of her shoes, holding out a frozen pizza.

Shadi attempts a smile. "That's really kind of you. Thanks."

They share the meal on the sofa, TV on. Shadi is still in her pyjamas. Anna has wrapped herself in a blanket, and occasionally she turns her head and stares almost dreamily across the harbour. Shadi follows her gaze. A row of cranes borders the right bank, as the setting sun casts a coral-tinted light across the water.

"Imagine being able to look at this every day," Anna murmurs, mouth full of pizza.

Under normal circumstances, Shadi would have thought much more carefully about what they're actually eating, but today she doesn't care. So what if she gets sick. It doesn't make any difference. She is, however, dreading the moment Anna gets up to go home.

"Are you thinking about Emil?"

Shadi shrugs. She'd like to explain to Anna that she and Emil have slept in the same bed every single night since they moved in. That no matter how late he stayed out he always came home, that she needs his breathing to stabilize her own.

"It's weird," she says. "I keep forgetting he isn't going to walk through the door at any moment. Then it hits me and I remember it all over again."

"Sounds a bit like when someone dies," says Anna. "It's like you have to keep comprehending it again and again."

Shadi wants to ask how she knows, but then decides it's none of her business. "What about you?" she asks instead. "Are you with anybody?"

Anna shakes her head. "I've started seeing someone, but it's early days." Her face changes as she answers, a softness that appears around her mouth.

"You look like you're in love," says Shadi. She sounds sad, although she doesn't mean it that way.

"Yeah, well, I definitely like her. But I haven't even been over to her place yet, so I'd say there's a way to go before it's a proper relationship."

Anna stretches and yawns. It's happening, Shadi fears. She's going to leave.

"You mind if I stay the night?"

And it's like being rescued from the brink. As though the corners of the apartment retreat back to the edges, now that Anna's staying. "Yeah, sure," Shadi says, getting quickly to her feet so Anna doesn't see how relieved she is. "I'll get some sheets and stuff."

ANNA

WHEN SHE OPENS HER EYES the next morning and looks straight out across the water, it's every bit as lovely as she thought it would be. Like lying on a raft in the middle of reflected cloud.

She smiles at Shadi, who's blinking next to her. "Did you sleep well?"

Shadi nods. Close up, Anna can see the fine down on her skin.

"It's really nice of you to come see people in crisis," Shadi mumbles, stretching. Anna thinks about her father and the way she left him last, with a weak excuse and the taste of shame under her tongue. Some guardian angel.

"I was just pissed off with you because you stood me up," she says. "But then I realized you hadn't put anything in the Dropbox folder for several days, and when you weren't picking up the phone either I had to see if you were okay."

"So, half nice, half pissed off?"

Shadi's cautious smile makes Anna laugh. "Yeah, that sounds like me!"

In the bathroom Anna tries every single one of Shadi's products, from the coconut lotion to the purple hair mask, and by the time she's done, the air is heavy with steam. Swaddling herself in the enormous towel Shadi has put out for her, she opens the first cabinet. Of course it's not cool, of course you're not supposed to go through other people's things, but she does it anyway. Every time. Once in a while she's surprised, like with that guy in Viby and his bathroom cabinet full of hash, but mostly the contents fit the owners, and by now she can compile a frighteningly accurate psychological profile based solely on a person's bathroom.

Shadi's place is painfully clean, no surprises there, and with a collection of unopened products neatly arrayed in the cabinet. On the glass shelf below the mirror is an indulgent face cream, and Anna scoops out a generous dollop, knowing that Shadi would hate it if she saw. That's when she opens the drawer underneath the sink.

There are two boxes. The one with the purple stripes she recognizes from when she was on the pill herself; the other is white with a red stripe and the name Cipralex. Maybe this Emil guy forgot them? She turns the packet over. No. It's Shadi's name on the label.

She sits down on the toilet lid, slightly bemused. One pill per day to combat anxiety and OCD, it says, and she skims the enclosed leaflet. One pill per day of a drug that might give Shadi anything from mood disorders and cramps to uterine bleeding. Carefully she refolds the leaflet and tucks it back into the box. Anxiety and OCD? Obviously Shadi's a bit uptight, and yeah, she does seem anxious sometimes. But Anna's never seen her do anything that resembles a compulsion, at least as far as she can recall.

The towel she has wrapped around her head has started tugging at her roots, so she leans forward and unwinds it. What should she do now? Tell Shadi she's been poking through her things? It would be a relief to get it out in the open, and there's a lot she'd like to ask. How she can bring herself to take something that alters her brain chemistry, for instance. Is this why she's so keen on the medical-industrial complex? On the other hand, Shadi seems really upset about Emil, and if there's one thing Anna has learned from Isam's coaching, it's that timing is everything. No reason to kick Shadi when she's already down.

She sits there for another few minutes with the box in her hands, trying to imagine how old Shadi was when she first went to the doctor and asked for help, how bad she must have felt to make that choice. Then, putting it back in the drawer, she picks up her things and opens the door with her elbow, stepping out in a cloud of coconut steam. Shadi is on the sofa with her legs folded beneath her and a large green teacup in her hands. At that moment she looks so peaceful that Anna knows she won't say anything about the pills. Not now, at any rate.

December 2015

——

ELISABETH

MUCH OF THE TIME ELISABETH looked after the mice herself; in fact, she insisted on it, even though they had techs for that sort of thing. She knew some of the others said behind her back that she was a control freak, the type of person who wanted to do everything herself for fear that no one else was good enough. They were fundamentally correct, but as a general rule she had no problem delegating mindless routine jobs. The truth was that she had recently become aware of something that no one else could, under any circumstances, be allowed to find out.

She had let a group of female mice reproduce, in order to see whether the latest formula might suppress their fertility or cause birth defects, and at first everything had looked fine. The mice gave birth, on average, to the same number of young as the unmedicated control groups. Yet not long after the litters were born, she began to sense that not everything was as it should be. The pups weren't gaining weight as quickly as normal, and the longer she watched, the more obvious it became why. Some of the mothers were simply not interested in their offspring. She stood in front of the cages and observed them as they washed, groomed their whiskers, and ate, apparently unmoved by the sound of their blind pups, which crowded together in squeaking huddles.

Those mothers licked their offspring less frequently, spent fewer minutes with them per day, and were overall less social than they should have been, and the discovery made a tiny, quivering tic appear by Elisabeth's right eye. There was something repellent about the whole scene, but it took her several days to work out why. It was motherhood. It was the pups' total dependency and the mothers' rejection that made her stomach turn.

She went back to her office and shut the door behind her, but the squealing pups had lodged inside her skull. What did it mean? Elisabeth was taking exactly the same medication as the mice, but the list of side effects in her notebook mentioned nothing about a lack of interest in her offspring, because how could she possibly have known? It was impossible to say what kind of mother she would be now—or what kind of daughter or wife or friend, for that matter. She was none of those things. The behaviour of the mice raised a question she was obliged to take seriously: Were the same disruptions to normal cognitive functioning in the rodents happening on some level to her as well? Had she overlooked something?

She rubbed her palms over her face, sitting up straight in her chair. She wrote down everything she felt. If anything about her had changed, she would have noticed. In any case, she still had years to take action. Even if the medication really was affecting the mice's ability to form bonds, she still had time to fix it. If, on the other hand, it came out now, during this study, the development of her miracle drug would be set back years; worst-case scenario, it would go down in Danish Pharma's history as yet another expensive waste of time. She couldn't let that happen.

Unfortunately, it was next to impossible to cheat at this level. The various results were meticulously noted, everything from the mice's weight to their reaction speeds, the number of seconds they spent playing and not playing, their sleep patterns. Everything was observed. Luckily the experiment was blind, so nobody knew which mice were being given the drug and which were controls, and although people at the lab had started muttering warily about some of the mice's antisocial behaviour, nobody could know for sure until the day the code was broken. So Elisabeth massaged her ticking eye muscle and racked her brain with steadily increasing desperation, trying to work out what she should do. Until, one day, the only possible solution appeared to her at last.

CHAPTER NINE

September 2024

————

SHADI

IN A WAY SHADI IS relieved when Anna goes and she can be herself again, but the second the door bangs, the thoughts about Emil come surging back. He's texted twice since yesterday, asking her to call so they can talk it out. *I miss you*, the last one said, and the words are an obsessive thought in their own right, impossible to sever from herself.

She begins an answer several times, edits and deletes and starts from scratch, until she can't bear herself anymore. Then she texts that she needs to think, that she'll call when she's ready. Then she stands quite still and waits, her pulse booming. At last, the message comes. A sole three words.

She can still remember the first time he said it. At the start, when they first began to see each other and she had to work out how to share herself with someone else, she was always on the

hunt for hiding places. Hurrying out the door ahead of him at her
parents' place and handing him the key so he could lock up, calling
her restrictive eating pickiness. When they slept together she lay
awake, waiting for him to drift off. Then she twisted free of his
arms, slunk into the kitchen, and stood there in the darkness with
her hand outstretched above the stove. Lowering it over and over
to the cold metal to convince herself that it was off. That nobody
would die that night. But it was so gruelling, hiding from him like
that, and one day she broke down. Now he's going to leave me, she
thought, her face in her hands; now he'll see how crazy I am. But
Emil had gripped her by the shoulders so firmly it had almost hurt,
and said he could tell she was struggling.

"I love you," he had said. "I'll take care of you. And I'm not
going anywhere."

Until now she's been dumb enough to believe it was true.

Without replying she starts to make the apartment her own again
after Anna's visit. Changing the sheets, tidying the bathroom, vac-
uuming the floors. In the end all that's left is the kitchen, but that's
also the worst. The sink with the sour milk, and the stove, where
Anna spilled egg this morning.

As she scours the dried-on stains, she remembers all the things
she imagined about that stove when they moved in. That she would
forget to switch it off and the neighbour with her two small kids
would burn alive, or that the old lady with the rabbit on the floor
above would die of smoke inhalation. The thoughts were so real,
and every day she had to set aside more time to turn back on her
way to class and return to check.

The stove has long since lost its power over her. So many of
her knots have loosened since Emil first took her to consult with
Annemette, and yet he's chosen now to be unfaithful. How does
that make sense? It would be easier to understand if he'd left
her straightaway, as soon as she'd shown him who she was. But
maybe that isn't how these things happen. She scrubs and scrubs,
although all trace of egg is gone and the sponge is beginning to

crumble into green flakes between her fingers. Perhaps it's built up over time inside Emil, the way a single grain of sand can turn into a heap without you ever knowing quite when it occurred.

Small, incremental changes, another call at work, another reassurance that the door is locked, without either of them realizing what it was doing to them. She'd rather that than believe he was only putting up with her, until the day he couldn't fake it anymore. That he knew it wouldn't work but didn't say. That would be worst of all.

ANNA

"JUST TURN OFF THE RICE and leave it to stand under the lid until we need it," says Siri. That's how she is, used to being right, swift to take charge. The type of person who has brought her own wine twice now, because that's the one she'd rather drink. But she can also be easygoing and bright.

"Climate?" she'd asked when Anna said she was vegetarian.

"Animal welfare," Anna had replied. "Having the power doesn't mean you get to act like an asshole."

Siri laughed and suggested they make dhal. She's good in the kitchen. Sautéing the dried spices with finely diced chili and ginger and pouring lentils into the dented IKEA pan without needing a recipe, while Anna washes coriander and cabbage from the supermarket. She'd forgotten how good home-cooked food can smell.

"So how does it work, then, when you're a lawyer?" she asks later as they're eating. "Do you specialize in anything?"

"You could say that. At first I was interested in intellectual property, but now I work more broadly on contracts and stuff like that."

"But what do you actually do?" It's hard to translate Siri's words into something she can picture. "Like on a totally normal, boring Monday?"

Siri's eyes flit upwards as she's thinking. "There are a bunch of meetings where I check each clause and make sure everything is being done by the book. I'm also often the one travelling to meet with our partners or accompanying the boss as a legal consultant."

Several times she tries to change the subject, but Anna isn't done. She wants to know if Siri likes what she does—if she's never wanted anything else. She has trouble reconciling this Siri with the one who makes sure the *i*'s are dotted and the *t*'s crossed on everybody else's ideas. There's so much more wildness in her than that; she's a leader, not a stickler for the rules. But Siri grins and says she gets plenty of opportunities to do the things she likes best.

"Law is just a mould we try to fit the world into, but the world is no less complex for that. I'm fine where I am," she says, nudging Anna's foot under the table. "What about you, I guess you're going to get out there and save us all when you're done?"

Anna shrugs. She honestly has no idea what she wants to do with her degree, only that it would be silly not to finish it now that she's come this far. "Sometimes I think I should have studied something else," she says. "Psychology is all right, but a lot of the theories are just so confusing. Then there's the whole debate over what works best therapeutically, it's so stupid."

She keeps talking, the wine buzzing pleasantly at the back of her head, but then Siri starts asking about her dissertation. About why she chose to write about grief and how come she's so against the new diagnosis, and something about the way she's asking causes a shift in the atmosphere.

"So, you think it's a good idea, diagnosing grief?" asks Anna. She doesn't know why she's so surprised, but she supposes she'd thought they would agree.

"Yeah, why not? Isn't it just a way of making it easier to talk about?" Siri ladles out some more dhal. "To create a common language, I mean?"

"We've got plenty of words," Anna protests. "Literature is full of descriptions of grief, or just look at the Bible, if you're into that. Existential thinking is all about death. I don't see the point of slapping on a clinical label."

"Well, we can't always let our emotions run the show, can we now?" says Siri, and she sounds so condescending that Anna has to clench her spoon so she won't say something she'll regret. "Sometimes we need a more objective way of talking about things if we want to professionalize them—it doesn't necessarily make much difference to ordinary people."

"But that's exactly the point!" Anna exclaims. "The people who dictate the language wield the power; the words we use mean everything. Haven't you ever read Foucault?"

She wishes she could take the last bit back. It makes her sound like she's only just heard about post-structuralism, so green and self-righteous. But she clamps her lips shut, and Siri doesn't say anything else. A few minutes later she gets to her feet. Anna can see her shoulder blades moving through the thin fabric of her blouse as she scrapes the food into the garbage and starts to clean up.

"Do you think I'm too much?" Anna's been down this road before, and if this is how it's going to be, they might as well rip the band-aid off now.

Siri turns toward her, soap bubbles crackling like static interference in her hands. "I think you're sweet," she says.

"Naive, you mean."

"No, I mean sweet." And holding out her arms to Anna, she drips two uneven trails of water across the floor.

THORSTEN

"SO, HOW'S THE WRITING GOING?" Thorsten asks.

He'd prefer not to beat around the bush, really, but Shadi was even more silent and timorous than usual during the few minutes they had to wait for Anna, so it seems like a good idea to start soft. Again, he tries to catch her eye, but her gaze is fixed on the floor, and Anna is the one who answers.

"It's going fine," she says. "I'm reading about the grief test. Isn't that demanding a lot from people's insight into themselves?"

It sounds like the classic objection to introspection, and as she keeps talking Thorsten's mind wanders back to the favour he was planning to ask Shadi. He was taken aback, he must admit, by her sudden offer to help with the stats. He'd been quietly thinking she was the one who'd benefit from collaborating with Anna, but perhaps he underestimated her. The thing is, though, that so far, he's marked two of her essays, and each one has been missing something. She always backs up her claims and has an unimpeachable grasp of the material, but her writing is too controlled for Thorsten's taste. There's a lack of reflection, of skin in the game—of life, frankly. Anna is the other way around, of course, flinging herself into her writing with a wildness that sometimes threatens to tip over. Her style is still untutored, and she would always rather speak than write. But she's inspired. Thorsten likes to think she has the ability, like the best blues musicians, to play the scale aslant, and that's what makes her perspective so interesting.

"Thorsten?"

He blinks and focuses sharply on the hand Anna is waving in front of his face.

"Were you even listening? You're miles away."

"Yes, I think I was," he confesses, glancing sidelong at Shadi, who is fiddling with a slender golden ring. He hopes he isn't making a mistake here. There's nothing wrong with sharing background material or the more superficial gloss that's in Anton's handout, but to give his students access to the personal data underneath it is, after all, a different and more serious matter.

"Shadi," he says, "do you remember what we talked about last time you were here? About the statistics?"

Finally she looks up.

"Do you still want to help? I know it's outside the remit of your dissertation, but perhaps some of it could prove useful for you two as well."

"I'd love to."

It's worth a study in itself, observing the transformation taking place. Her body straightens in her seat, and her eyes, which until now have been glassy, grow animated.

"Sorry," Anna says, putting up her hand, "but is anybody going to explain to me what's going on?"

Thorsten smiles at Shadi. It's never been easy for Anna not to be the centre of attention. "There's something about our grief project that's baffled me," he explains. "And Shadi offered to take a quick look for me. Tech stuff isn't exactly my strong suit, you know."

At that remark Anna gives a shout of laughter that's a bit too loud for Thorsten's liking. Holding up a pointed index finger she imitates him sweating over the keyboard, and even Shadi smiles now.

"Yes, yes, thank you." Thorsten raises his hands in surrender. "I'll send you the data set, then," he says to Shadi. "I'd like you to start with the scores that were left out, please. Our statistician Anton called them something…"

"Outliers?"

"That's the one. Maybe you can tell me if it made sense to remove them, and also it would be a big help if you could rerun the most important of Anton's calculations. The changes in empathy over time in the two groups, the improvement in the subjects who were given Callocain."

"Sure," says Shadi, and adds a little shyly, "if I can."

"Right." Anna claps her palms together with a decisive smack. "If Shadi's going rogue, then I think I might go a bit off myself. Gather some inspiration, get away from the books and all that."

"Sometimes I think your entire academic career has been about getting away from the books," Thorsten remarks. "Where to, might I ask?"

"Danish Pharma. I've written and asked if I can come and visit, but they didn't reply. Might be easier if I just go there."

He nods. "I'm sure it's fine to gather some background on the development of Callocain. We've had their head of research at a couple of our meetings, Elisabeth Nordin. You can ask for her."

January 2016

ELISABETH

WHEN IT CAME TIME TO pool the results from the medicated mice and the controls, Elisabeth made sure she was the one to break the code, doing it late one night when she was the only person there. Over the years she had built up such a good reputation that nobody would wonder why she, as head of research, had done it with no witnesses present. They trusted she would carry out her work in an ethically responsible fashion, and that the various security precautions would take care of the rest. She had never given them any reason to think otherwise.

The nerve by her eye went berserk when she broke the blind and saw which mice had received the drug and which had not. It wasn't quite as bad as she'd feared, but the difference was indisputable. A number of the medicated mice had simply become bad mothers; several of their young died within the first few weeks, while others were underweight and frail. From earlier experiments with pups that hadn't received the attention and care they were naturally due after birth, she knew that if they were allowed to live, they would grow up to become bad mothers themselves, forming conflict-ridden relationships with their fellow mice. In other words, she had unwittingly conducted a study on insecure attachment.

Elisabeth sat for a long time in front of the screen, the blood rushing in her veins. The results were plain, yet she could hardly believe them. She had kept herself under intense scrutiny over the past weeks, but still observed no sign that her own social skills had been affected by the medication. After all, she had started withdrawing from the few relationships she did have immediately after Winter's death, so she couldn't blame the pills for that. In fact, she felt instead that she was gradually returning to her original state, before life as a mother. She was a loner by nature.

Maybe this was a behavioural change that occurred only in mice, and it wouldn't transfer across to humans in the same way. An unfortunate side effect that would have no real significance once the pills were in the right hands. It was certainly a possibility, but, regardless, she had to solve the problem in front of her if they were going to move forward with the trials. Still, she hesitated. This was the first time in her career she had crossed the line so definitively between right and wrong, and it was more of a struggle than she'd thought. What she was about to do was so serious that even a trace of suspicion would see her kicked out of Danish Pharma and discredited so thoroughly that she would never work in the industry again. More than that—it just felt wrong, even though she promised herself that she would sort it out long before the pills ever got anywhere near a pharmacy. That this was necessary if she was going to realize her dream.

Her fingertips whirled, then her hands dropped from the keyboard and she went to stand by the window. It helped a bit to think back to their first animal trials. They had begun by inducing a kind of correlate to grief, taking away the mice's young and stressing them by moistening the floors in their cages. Then they had divided the mice into one group on Callocain, one on antidepressants, and one without any medication at all, and tested them; she still remembers how ecstatic they had been when the results came through. How the grieving mice on Callocain continued to swim in the basin long after the others had given up, and how quickly they learned the way through the labyrinth. The trial overall had been a huge success, and the first real indication they had produced a drug that might change the world. Shouldn't that be what she remembered now? How many grieving people she could potentially help to live better lives? Should she really let a few selfish mice and a trend that was far from pronounced—and which she would work day and night to eliminate—ruin all that?

She sat back down at the screen, running her hands just once over her pants to get rid of the clamminess. And then she did it.

She opened the list and moved half the numbers from one column into the second and the other way around, jumbling the medicated mice with the controls. When she—and, later, their statisticians—got to work the next morning, the discrepancies between the groups would have magically adjusted, and although the spread would be unusually wide, that sort of thing did happen. Everyone, herself included, could breathe a sigh of relief. It would be time to terminate the mice and start to plan experimental protocols for the logical next step: human beings.

CHAPTER TEN

September 2024

———

ANNA

"I'm afraid I can't see an appointment in my calendar—with Elisabeth or anybody else. I'll have to ask you to write an email and book a meeting, then you'd be more than welcome to come back."

The secretary at Danish Pharma is friendly yet somehow dismissive, and it would be fascinating if it wasn't so goddamn annoying.

"That's what I'm trying to tell you." Anna leans over the steel desk. "I've written a bunch of times, and you guys are the ones not replying. And now I'm working on this big study at Aarhus University, which includes a critical analysis of the grief diagnosis and the drug you've developed, so it would be kind of a shame if you didn't get to present your side."

They stare each other down.

"I'm also lucky enough to have a few friends who make documentaries for national television who are very interested in my perspective on the whole idea of getting rid of grief with pills."

The lie hovers in the air between them like a glinting soap bubble, and Anna knows she's won when the secretary purses her lips and reaches sour-faced for the phone.

As it turns out, the person who has time to speak to a pushy student is named Lars, and he looks at once too young and too nice to be squared with Anna's prejudices. He produces a cup of creamy coffee and ushers her down high-ceilinged corridors. As they walk, he tells her about how Danish Pharma was founded, and how the first hundred employees have swelled to ten thousand within just a few years.

"This is where Elisabeth sits," he says, nodding toward a vast, empty office, "when she's here. But she's a busy lady, so you'll have to settle for me today."

Lars's own office is almost as large and elegant, and it's hard not to feel out of place with her cropped jeans and cheap home dye-job. Maybe that's why she goes in so hard.

"There's so much about your development of Callocain that's problematic," Anna begins, once she's set her phone to record. "Let's start with the premise itself: that grief is something we need to cure. I mean, that seems absurd to me on its face."

"Listen, Anna," says Lars, and for the first time he looks grave. "I can well understand that you're passionate about your dissertation, and I'd love to talk to you about the thinking behind Callocain. Persistent grief is an important topic, and we take it very seriously here at Danish Pharma, okay?"

Anna shrugs, trying to relax.

"So, I think it's vital to establish a few facts straight off the bat. We are not treating grief. What Callocain *can* help with is the long-term, pathological condition some people experience when they lose someone they love. That's persistent grief disorder. And here the research shows, as I'm sure you know, that people can really struggle if they don't get support. We're talking social problems, severe mental illness, suicidal ideation and so on, and when a death leads to such severe consequences, then yes, we do think it's our obligation to help."

He smiles again and leans back in his chair, so fucking slick—and in the moment all Anna can come up with is, "Fair enough."

"Great!"

Lars laughs; how old is this guy? He doesn't look a day over thirty.

"So, let's say it is a good idea to help people if they're grieving for too long." Anna sets down her cup and wipes the moisture from her upper lip. "But there are already other diagnoses to describe that—post-traumatic stress disorder, for instance. Why not just use those?"

"Well, we're not the ones making the diagnoses," Lars replies. "But there's substantial evidence to indicate that a disordered response to grief is different from other illnesses, both physiologically and phenomenologically. For example, antidepressants are significantly less effective at treating grief than treating ordinary depression."

"So, you genuinely believe it makes sense to view grief as a mental illness?" Anna asks, and the man-child in front of her nods.

"As a pharmaceutical company, we only start working on a new drug once we're sure there's a specific biological correlate to the symptoms. In layman's terms, if we don't know what's going wrong in the brain, we can't develop the right treatment. And it does indeed appear that persistent grief disorder has a clear neurological correlate."

"But why a pill? The research shows, as I'm sure you're aware—" here Anna is careful to use exactly the same pattern of emphasis as he did a moment earlier "—that psychotherapy has no side effects. Unlike more or less every drug that has ever been made."

Lars evidently can't make up his mind whether to find her amusing or annoying. He narrows his eyes, but the smile is still there. It's just like Muay Thai, thinks Anna: you circle around, feint, jab. Constantly on the hunt for the right moment to strike.

"As it stands, your profession makes quite a good living off the bereaved," says Lars. "As soon as having a dead relative made people eligible for treatment on the national health service, that opened up access to 200,000 more clients. But because we're supplying pills instead of therapy sessions—which also, at base, are a way of attempting to alter a person's brain chemistry—for some reason the pharmaceutical companies are always the bad guys. Yes, we make money off what we make, but I can't see how that makes us any different from psychiatrists or psychologists or anybody else who works in mental health."

The man has a point, but she has no intention of saying so.

"Do you know how long it takes to go from the initial idea for a new drug to launching the finished product onto the market?" he asks.

She shakes her head. "Seven years?"

"Fifteen!" He gazes at her intently. "Ten to fifteen years. From the first tentative experiments in the lab to the day we can finally begin testing microscopic amounts of the drug on human beings, that can be four or five years, and lots of excellent ideas run aground along the way. Our products may seem expensive, but it's because we rely on the vanishingly small number of drugs that make it through the elimination process to keep this whole place running." He throws out his arms.

Anna thinks of the enormous lobby, the deep aroma of the coffee. "I wouldn't exactly call Arne Jacobsen furniture a human right," she says. Lars laughs again, his forehead glistening under his wavy hair. She gives him a smile despite herself. He's probably decent enough, just a cheery foot soldier who's drunk the company Kool-Aid. Still, that doesn't mean she won't strike if she gets the chance. "We agree nobody is keeping an eye on you during the development process, correct?"

He frowns. "What do you mean?"

"There's no impartial body—the university, for instance, or the Danish Medicines Agency—involved in the development of your pills, right?"

"That's correct. But we have no incentive to put out a drug that doesn't work, or that has serious side effects. It would be tantamount to suicide not to make sure our products stand up to scrutiny."

"It's one thing to deliberately deceive people," says Anna, "but after you've sunk ten years and who knows how many millions into developing a product, how unbiased do you think you are when it comes to assessing it?"

"Oh, but our trials are randomized, controlled, and double-blind," Lars protests. "All our observations are input into a special database that ends up with the Danish Medicines Agency, and it's impossible for us to change. It's an incredibly thorough and secure process."

"Sure. But we both know that people with a vested interest in something—financially, say—have a tendency to warp the way they collect, record, and process information." The words coming out of her mouth are Thorsten's; she's heard him say them so many times. "And there are reams of studies documenting that both doctors and test subjects are often fully aware of whether they're taking chalk or medication, not least because placebos virtually never cause side effects. So, if you don't get a dry mouth or worse, you're most likely in the placebo group. In which case, so much for the blinding."

Knockout, she thinks, at least a little one. Lars keeps talking, of course, raising his arms and gesturing wildly to show how wrong she is. But Anna can sense it; she knows that prickle in her bones. The way it feels when a punch hits home.

THORSTEN

THE RING TONE ON THORSTEN'S new work phone, which is so smart it's almost impossible to figure out, startles him out of his preparations for an upcoming conference in Stockholm. It's Marianne, the departmental secretary.

"I've got an Erik Svensson on the line," she says. "Married to Vibeke from the grief project. He's asking for Miguel, but he's not here today. Do you have a minute?"

"Just put him through," says Thorsten, flipping through the pile of patient notes with his free hand, looking for Vibeke's name.

"Yes, hello." The voice in his ear is a low rumble. "It's about the trial you're running, the one my wife is participating in. I have a few questions about the treatment."

At last Thorsten finds the right page in the file. It's as he thought. Vibeke is the middle-aged woman who was adopted from a Russian orphanage when she was little, along with her twin, Eva. For years after the sisters arrived in Denmark, they had trouble forming relationships with anyone outside their sibling bubble, and as Thorsten understands it, Eva lived with Vibeke and Erik until her death last year. The twins did everything together, and when Eva died, Vibeke became convinced she must be sick as well, that it was only a matter of time before she died too. But the doctors examined every inch of her and declared that she was in perfect health. After that, she sank into the darkness that had made her husband contact the grief project.

"It's not that I'm ungrateful," says Erik. "I hope you understand that. My wife has been feeling much better since the trial started. But I have to say I'm looking forward to when it finishes."

"Oh, really?"

Thorsten leafs through to the last grief questionnaire he did with Vibeke. Six points, a huge improvement from the thirteen she scored the first time he saw her.

"Yes, I mean, I assume she won't have to keep taking those pills?"

Thorsten reassures him that that's definitely not the plan. "You stop taking Callocain once you're feeling better," he explains, "and in our case we taper all our participants off the medication when the study is over, regardless of whether they've been given a placebo or active treatment. There may be some leeway for certain individuals as to how fast we do that, but it's up to Miguel."

"That's good," says Erik. "After a while you start to want your wife back."

Thorsten frowns. He jots down the sentence out of sheer force of habit. *After a while you start to want your wife back.* "How do you mean?"

"Well." Erik pauses. "I think she's become a bit distant. Spends a lot of time alone, you know, goes hunting quite a bit and so on."

Thorsten skims through his notes, but he hasn't written down anything very striking during his meetings with Vibeke. Only that she seemed to be making progress. Which, on the face of it, would make sense if she was in the Callocain group, but of course he can't be sure.

"She really likes the pills," Erik continues. "Only yesterday she was saying that if you wouldn't keep prescribing them to her, she'd find a psychiatrist who would." The bass intensifies. "And if I say I miss her, or that I don't think she's really herself, she looks at me like I'm an idiot and asks who the hell's their usual self after losing their sister. And the conversation ends there."

Thorsten promises he'll ask Miguel to get in touch with them as soon as possible. "I'm sure he'll come up with a good plan for Vibeke," he says, "whether she was on the medication or it turns out she's feeling better naturally. And please tell her she can always call if she needs to speak to me about anything. Any time."

After they've hung up, Thorsten sits holding the phone in his hand. How much credence should he lend to Erik's complaint? After all, it's been less than eighteen months since Vibeke lost perhaps the most important person in her life. What looks to Erik like disengagement might for Vibeke be a process of reflection, or an attempt to re-establish meaning. Still, he can't help but be reminded of Mikkel and his oddly distanced account of the fact that his family has been taken from him. And regardless, he doesn't think much of Vibeke's plan to keep taking the drug. Even if she's right about being on Callocain, even if it really has helped, it's not meant to be taken for that long.

On an impulse he starts combing through her test sheet as carefully as he went through Mikkel's. Not only did she drop to a seven in the most recent EQ assessment, but she's also one of the eight subjects on his list of strikingly steep nosedives. All the more crucial, he thinks, that they properly taper her off the drug. If her empathy score is even remotely connected to the medication, then in his opinion it would be decidedly reckless to continue treatment.

SHADI

AS SOON AS SHADI GETS back from the university, she clicks on Thorsten's email. The first file is the overview she's supposed to transfer into SPSS. She's never worked with real data from a research project before, but actually putting together a set is easy once you know the system. Basically, all you have to do is convert any information that isn't already numerical into digits. Previous mental illness is a 1, no known illness a 0. Their various levels of education she assigns a number from 1 to 6, continuing in the same fashion down each row. Numbers are the language the program speaks, and her job is to make the communication as precise as possible.

She hasn't used SPSS much since the course, and she'd almost forgotten how much she loves it. The ruler-straight striae of information, the knowledge that everything will fall into place so long as she types it all in properly. The deep satisfaction of bringing order to chaos. Hours pass almost without her noticing, and when at last she leans back, she has a complete data set. It's the longest she's gone without thinking of Emil since he left.

She starts out with a couple of simple tasks, just to warm up. Typing in the commands and asking the program to check whether there is a correlation between the age and grief score. And boom, in a split second the calculation is done. No correlation. Feeling a little more confident, she inquires about the connection between two things that should be connected: the grief score and a test of the participants' memory. This time she chooses to view the result as a scatter plot, and the correlation is obvious. The more symptoms the participants exhibited, the worse they were at recalling a story that had been read to them. So far, so familiar. Again she skims the file containing Anton's results. There's nothing about which specific tests he used, but a t-test would make the most sense if she's going to compare the treatment group with the placebo. And then she realizes. It's only just dawned on her that she has no idea which of the nearly four hundred numbers on the list were given Callocain and which were not. The actual key to the set is missing!

She reads scrupulously through all the emails and attachments Thorsten has ever sent her, but they're no help at all. It isn't there. Frustrated, she shuts the laptop. Without that information, it's impossible to do as he's asked. Darkness has fallen in the flat without her noticing, and she gets up on stiff legs. Switching on the hanging lamp above the desk, she fetches the honeydew melon Anna brought back from the shops and eats it standing at the kitchen table. Half past nine. What should she do now? Take an evening stroll with her hands swinging empty through the air, choose a film and watch it without Emil to nestle up against? She doesn't feel like any of that. So, she contents herself with checking the door the obligatory three times before she brushes her teeth and crawls under the duvet. And although she's afraid until the last second that she'll have trouble falling asleep again, that she will never truly sleep without Emil, it happens after all, something tugging at her, so that she falls and half awakens, only to fall once more.

April 2017

ELISABETH

IT'S IRRATIONAL, ELISABETH KNOWS, TAKING the dog for a walk beforehand, but somehow it made the most sense. One last trip to their old favourite spot by the lake, where Nala loved fetching sticks and digging in the damp wetland earth. One last splash through the shallow, muddy water, tail spinning like a propeller. She looked away; she couldn't bear anymore to look at the dog. Its plump, happy body, its eyes that demanded something she could no longer give.

The pills were on the table, waiting. She'd got hold of them through an acquaintance who was a vet. Two were enough, apparently, but she'd asked for three to be sure. When they got home from the walk, Nala lumbered contentedly onto the carpet with her stuffed toy, a chewed-up giraffe that squeaked feebly whenever the dog's jaws closed around its stomach. It felt sometimes as though the giraffe gave Nala an extra voice. Elisabeth would ask a question—where the TV remote had got to, or whether it was time to take a walk—and it was the giraffe that would squeak in reply.

Nala watched with interest as she prepared the bowl of food. Weren't they supposed to be able to sense when something was wrong? she thought, crushing the pills into the pâté. Weren't dogs experts in body language?

"How about we finish with something tasty, eh?"

The tail thumping against the chest of drawers, *thud, thud, thud*. The trusting eyes that never saw the bigger picture yet captured all the small ones.

"There we go."

She placed the bowl on the floor and the dog lunged for it, gulping down the food swiftly and eagerly, always as though it were the last meal it would ever have. Today it was right.

Afterward she considered what to do next. She felt strange, and ended up slumping onto the floor with her back to the wall.

Nala came over immediately, licked her hand, and lay down very close. They hadn't sat like that since she was a puppy. Nala had been Winter's dog, and he had loved her to the moon and back. She slept at his feet when he couldn't leave his bed, and it seemed there was no place the dog would rather be than where he was. "Here comes my son and his shadow," Elisabeth would say as her frail boy walked over with his furry friend at his heels. Sometimes she'd thought Nala might almost be too lively for Winter, so stark was the contrast between him and the bounding dog, full of a vitality her son had never possessed. Lately she had been consumed with the thought that a shadow made no sense without anyone to cast it. How could Nala keep existing in a world without Winter?

"I am fond of you, you know?" she whispered. "It's just, this can't go on."

Nala gave a happy, guttural growl, and she scratched behind the dog's ears. She stroked her spotted coat, brown and white with patches of black, running her hand over her soft head and along her body, all the way down her hind legs. Nala sighed and turned onto one side. The giraffe lay nearby, and the dog raised her head a few centimetres, as though considering whether to reach for the toy. Perhaps it was the look in her eyes, the naive surprise at being unable to complete the movement, that woke Elisabeth up. What was she doing? This was Nala, the only living being who had adored Winter as much as she had. Without knowing whether it was the right thing to do, she grabbed Nala's muzzle and opened its mouth. Stuck her fingers in between its jaws and groped around the roof of its mouth and its warm, wet tongue, but the dog kept wriggling free, and it was impossible to get the right spot.

"Come on, bring it up," she commanded, but although Nala gave a few hacking coughs, nothing came up. The dog's heavy head slipped to the carpet, and Elisabeth frantically wiped her slippery fingers on her sweater and grabbed her phone to search for how you made a dog throw up. But it was no use, the results were unusable. She was sobbing with frustration now, and beside her Nala sighed, almost as though falling asleep, almost as though one breath wouldn't suddenly prove to be the last, leaving only a limp dead body, yet another life Elisabeth had in her hands and then let slip.

CHAPTER ELEVEN

September 2024

———

ANNA

SIRI'S HANDS ARE GOOD. ANNA lies still, eyes closed, feeling the way her hands grasp peculiarly hard and yet don't hurt. They skim her body as though to trace its outline, and when at last it's bright and clear in her mind's eye, she raises herself up. Winds her legs around Siri so that they become one concerted movement.

"That's lovely," she murmurs. Siri presses her nose into her neck. Kisses her so it tickles down her spine.

"You're the lovely one."

They take a shower together. Afterwards, Anna opens the bedroom window, which is wet with condensation. Some kids are yelling in the street, and the aroma of barbecuing makes it feel like summer still.

"It's my friend's birthday on Thursday," she says, trying to sound casual. "She's rented a whole club."

"Mm," Siri hums from the bed.

"Want to come?"

But Siri has Anna's computer in her lap, and instead of answering she asks for the password so she can find a movie for them to watch.

"Nineteen ninety-nine."

Siri raises an eyebrow. "Please don't tell me that's the year you were born," she says, but Anna only laughs. Climbing onto the bed, she burrows up against Siri's body, which is still damp from the shower. "So are you coming, then?" she asks. "On Thursday?" She leans into Siri. It would be the first time meeting any of each other's friends.

"Maybe," says Siri, her eyes fixed on the screen. "We'll see."

The next morning Anna wakes alone in bed. Siri, she can hear, is busy in the kitchen. Last night, after she'd fallen asleep, Anna watched her trembling eyelids, her half-open mouth as it exhaled measured little puffs of air, thinking how glad she was that Siri was in her bed right now and no one else's. Her scent still is. It reminds her of pale green spring leaves and fresh-cut wood; not in a perfumed way, but as though the fragrance is Siri's own. As though she's come straight from the forest.

Still groggy, she puts on some clothes and looks for her phone. Usually she leaves it on the windowsill, but it isn't there. So she follows the noises: a spoon scraped against the side of a bowl, a cup being set a little too hard on the table. On the threshold she pauses. Is Siri the kind of person you kiss good morning, or is that too relationshippy?

"Morning." Siri smiles up at her. Her hair is big and curly and reminds Anna of the first time she saw her that day at the library. "Did you sleep well? You seemed a bit upset at one point."

This again. At first she'd cried herself awake pretty much every night, in the violent way that mostly only children do, but these days it's usually the bloodshot eyes that betray her in the mirror in the morning, every now and then. "Fine, thanks."

She smiles at Siri, who holds her gaze for a few seconds before nodding. Grateful that they don't need to get into all that, Anna flops down into a chair at the little folding table. At that moment she sets eyes on her phone, which is on the kitchen table. She must have left it there the night before.

"You got any plans today?" Siri hands her a cup of coffee.

"Nah, maybe do a bit of writing. I've been down to Danish Pharma."

"Oh?" Siri eyes her expectantly. She looks different like this, without makeup. Less hard. "Anything to report?"

Anna shrugs. "I was planning to write that grief is important because it says something about what we've lost. That if you drown it in meds, you can't process it properly. But the guy I talked to kept saying that it's not grief they're treating but the disorder it can turn into. Like, as though they're two completely different things. And now I don't know…"

Siri pauses, spoon halfway to her mouth. "What?" she asks.

"No, it's just…I was so sure about all this before I started."

Siri smiles. "Isn't that the whole point? It's not a bad thing to change your mind a little."

"I'm sure you think so," says Anna, "but I hate this idea that everything has to be fixed. Why can't they just let us be sad when someone dies?"

As she says the words her mouth curls, and it happens so abruptly that she can't even react. Siri puts out her hand, shocked, but Anna jerks to her feet and runs into the toilet. She grabs the sink to keep her balance, and before she can shut the door, Siri is behind her.

"Anna, what's going on?"

She shakes her head, trying to get her breathing under control.

Siri puts her hand on her upper arm. "Tell me what it is."

Anna can see them in the mirror. Her own pallid, waxen face and crying mouth, Siri's wide eyes. "My mother died."

The words she almost never says feel strangely nice to say to Siri. Like splitting something precious in two and holding out one half in her open palm.

"When?"

"In March, so that's…" she counts "…six months and twenty-five days ago now. But it doesn't usually affect me like this, I don't know why…"

Siri makes a reassuring sound and puts her arms around her. The gesture is so full of solace that Anna turns at once into her embrace.

THORSTEN

AT FIRST THORSTEN CAN'T BELIEVE his eyes; he flips through
Anton's handout for the tenth time and clicks through the database,
but Shadi is right. It doesn't say anywhere who is on the drug and
who is not. He shakes his head. Of course it doesn't. He doesn't
even know himself who's had what—he assumes only Anton and
possibly Kamilla have that information.

Frustrated, he slams his fist onto the desk. Without the code,
Shadi can't do what he's asked her to do. Where on earth do they
go from here?

At four o'clock precisely Thorsten knocks on the door of the borrowed office Miguel uses when he's at the university. The lanky
doctor flicks a cigarette butt out the window—management would
throw a fit.

"Just one. Clears the mind," he says, winking at Thorsten. "But
come in, come in! Help yourself." He gestures toward a bowl of
plums, which Thorsten knows from past experience he'd best avoid
if he doesn't want his allergies acting up. "There was something
you wanted to discuss?"

"Yes, please. It's about our joint project," Thorsten explains,
taking a seat. "I'd like to make sure I've understood this properly.
You're going to wean all our participants off the drug before we let
them loose, correct?"

Miguel nods. "In principle, yes."

"In principle?"

"People react differently to these things," explains Miguel. "Some
might backslide, maybe experience withdrawal symptoms or something else that means I don't have time to walk them through every
step. In which case they'll be referred back to their own doctors."

"Who'll then wean them off?" Thorsten persists. "Because I just
heard about one participant who believes she's had Callocain and
is talking about continuing treatment with a psychiatrist when
she's finished here. But I guess that won't happen?"

Miguel tilts his head from side to side, his shiny bald scalp mirroring the light of the ceiling lamp. "It's been known," he says. "If you're insistent enough and can find a doctor who thinks it's a good idea, then…" He smiles lopsidedly at Thorsten. "Just look at antidepressants. They were never meant to be prescribed for life, were they?"

Before Thorsten can respond, Svend appears in the doorway.

"Is this where the party's happening?" he asks, snuffling delightedly at the traces of tobacco smoke still lingering in the air.

"Not sure I'd call it a party," grunts Thorsten, turning back to Miguel. "I can't be the only one who's uncomfortable with allowing grieving people to become dissocial on our watch? Particularly if they end up on these pills for years, once Callocain is approved?"

He doesn't fail to notice the look Svend and Miguel exchange.

"You want to know what I think?" asks Svend. "I think you've gone off the deep end with this one."

"That's just because I haven't told you everything," Thorsten objects. "There are some things I'm keeping to myself for the time being, but—"

"You know what, I don't actually believe that," Svend interrupts. "There are seven other researchers on this project, and none of us sees it the way you do. Yes, their empathy scores have dropped a bit, and no, they haven't returned to normal yet, despite the fact that the participants are feeling better, but I'd bet you anything they will in a month or two. And in any case, it's something we should analyze professionally. As a team." He shakes his head. "All this rooting around for bad apples in your own research group, Thorsten, it's a bit much. I don't like it when you get like this."

When he gets like this? Something about the words reminds Thorsten of Kamilla. What had she said that day? *We're worried about you?*

"Tell me," he says, looking from Svend to Miguel and back, "have you been talking about me behind my back? Saying I'm some kind of conspiracy-minded idiot who's lost the plot, is that it?"

"Thorsten," Miguel says reassuringly, but Thorsten jumps to his feet.

"No," he says. "I mean it!"

"Jesus, Thorsten, can't you hear yourself?" Svend looks at him with sad eyes. "That's exactly the problem."

SHADI

"I'M SORRY ABOUT THE CODE," Thorsten blurts as soon as Shadi picks up the phone. "It completely slipped my mind. Nobody but Anton and Kamilla have access to it."

"Okay," she says. "But then what do we do?"

The lethargy is trapped like tiny bubbles of air against the inside of her skin. All those hours of work spent putting together the set in SPSS, the whole silly fantasy about being the smart student who solves her supervisor's academic riddle and saves the day. And she's missing the one column without which the others don't make sense.

"Isn't there anything you can do?" asks Thorsten. "Other calculations you could do instead?"

"Yeah, maybe, I guess. But all the things we want to know are about the effects of Callocain. Whether the drug makes people feel better, what the connection is between Callocain and empathy, all that stuff. And that's impossible if I don't know who's been given what. Everything is jumbled up."

"This is a godawful mess," says Thorsten. "Kamilla will be going to the press any day now if we don't come up with something to stop her. And once she's rubber-stamped Callocain, it's a matter of days before it hits the market. They've had approval from the authorities—it's just us they're waiting for now."

"I get that. I just don't know how I'm supposed to—"

"The outliers," Thorsten interrupts. "Did you take a look at those?"

"Yes. There were three, like you thought. And I don't understand why Anton removed them either. They're the three lowest, so of course they fall outside the rest, but there are other scores below ten."

"So they shouldn't have been removed?"

"It's hard to say, not knowing more. Could it be maybe because something went wrong during testing, so the results weren't good enough?"

"Well, only one of the test subjects was mine," he says, "but there was certainly nothing wrong with the way he was tested."

The low hiss on the line reminds Shadi of the sound of the sea through the windows during a storm.

"I'm afraid we're missing something here," says Thorsten quietly. "Something big that might have terrible consequences for the people involved."

Shadi swallows. "I'll try again," she hears herself say. "I'm not making any promises, but I will take another look."

"Thank you," he says. "And, Shadi?"

"Yes?"

"Hurry."

ANNA

ANNA IS SITTING ON THE windowsill, gazing out at the building opposite, which looks like a dropped Lego brick in all that grey. Yesterday it was a relief to tell Siri about her mother. Not today. She woke in heavy slow-motion and can't shake it off, and apart from complaining to the board about the neuro class she failed, she hasn't ticked off any of the things she wanted to get done. For the last few hours she's just been sitting here. Every now and then a face appears in one of the windows in the block, but nobody looks up high enough to catch sight of Anna. And when it strikes her that she could sit right there in her plaster box and die without any of them so much as noticing, she swings her legs down and lands on the floor. Something has to happen now, or this weight will carry over into tomorrow.

It's an effort to put her running gear on but she does it, and minutes later she's heading toward the woods. The dusk is even thicker in there, and all she can hear is her own laboured breathing. Every time she passes the exercise equipment on her circular route, she hoists herself up and does her usual five chin-ups, and by the time she turns back down Karen Blixens Boulevard three laps later, she's sheer body. Yet again, she's managed to run from something, which she's now left at the forest's edge.

After a shower she starts looking for the copy of the grief test Thorsten sent her. It was impossible to speak to him about it at the last supervision because he was so obsessed with getting Shadi to help with his grief project, so now she's got to do it herself. Take the test. Simple. This way works best for her anyhow, same as the visit to Danish Pharma. Later, when she sits down to write, she'll be able to hear Lars's words in her ear or recall a certain phrasing from the test, and it will make the words come that much easier.

It soon becomes apparent that she falls outside the test's general criteria. Yeah, so her pizza consumption may be too high and her running clothes are so salty they could stand up on their own, but she still has her shit together. Especially now she's got someone to keep her accountable. In other words, she's too high-functioning for the grief diagnosis to apply, and she likes that about it. That it doesn't actually fit everyone who's lost somebody. Still, she keeps going, trying to answer the questions as honestly as possible. Some of them are easy enough, others give her pause. Has she experienced a diminished sense of self, as though a part of her has vanished, since her mother died? Of course she has. There are ways that no one else can look at her, words she will never say in the same way to any other person. There are experiences they had together that are now up to Anna to carry forward. The rare moments when her mother agreed to sing her a lullaby, and her voice grew soft in a way it never did otherwise. Lying on the sofa with her head in her lap and having her back rubbed, even after Anna was too old for it really. And lately, recognizing her mother in her own laugh or one of her gestures, and knowing now that all of that is hers alone. But how she's supposed to figure out what impact that has had on her sense of self, she has no clue.

The next question is about whether she avoids certain things, places, or people because they remind her of the loss. Her first impulse is no: she decided long ago not to let herself be restricted by anything. But the thought of her father's drooping back stops her cold, and for a moment her hand wavers in the air, somewhere between yes and no. Then she shoves the computer away and goes into the kitchen. It's a stupid test. She opens the fridge and stares into the empty space. It's not like it applies to her anyway, so why waste so much as a second more on it?

July 2019

ELISABETH

AS A RULE ELISABETH HATED these get-togethers at Danish Pharma—the obligatory New Year's bash, the recurring summer party—and for the most part she stayed away. This time, however, Marcus had been unusually insistent, so now she was standing around with a few other people from the team on the wide lawn behind the main building, trying to unwind. The sun was burning her shoulders in her strappy red dress; come to think of it, it was probably the first time this summer she had been outside without being on her way to somewhere else. Just then, somebody tapped a glass.

"May I have your attention for a moment?"

It was Marcus, looking every inch what he was, in his tailored trousers and dazzlingly white shirt: the boss. Slowly people gathered around him, and the chatter died down.

"What a magnificent setting," he began, throwing out his arms in an all-encompassing gesture. "And I don't think I'd be lying if I said that the future of our little company is looking about as cloudless as the sky we're lucky enough to be enjoying today. There is one particular person I'd like to thank for that." He found Elisabeth's gaze and jerked his head, beckoning her closer. "The woman behind one of the most promising projects I have witnessed in a very long time. We're not home free yet, I know that, but, ladies and gentlemen, Elisabeth and the rest of her fantastic team have just brought the development of Callocain safely into phase three. What do you say to that?"

Elisabeth walked up to Marcus and took the long-stemmed glass he offered her. There was clapping, and as she made sure to smile, her eyes swept across her colleagues, who were dressed to the nines. Who were all these people with whom she spent so many of her waking hours? Sofia and the rest of the team, the doctors and biologists, that pasty-faced statistician who had wisely gone to stand in the shade? What difference did any of it make to her?

She certainly deserved to be singled out by Marcus this year. Although much of her work took place behind closed doors, tucked away in the lab or sheltering behind a computer screen, she was sure that out of all the people in the garden she had put the most hours into her research, and she was the driving force behind what was bound to be one of the company's greatest triumphs. The irony was that the whole masquerade felt completely devoid of meaning. All she could think about while Marcus rambled on about the company's bright prospects was Nala. The dog would have been thirteen today, no doubt stiff-legged and slow on the stairs, but for some reason she was absolutely convinced it would still be alive if she hadn't killed it that day on the kitchen floor.

She would have come home that evening, would have stepped through the door and out of her dress, and Nala would have come up to meet her as she always did, tail wagging, eager to lick her hands. She would have crouched down to stroke the dog's soft coat, and perhaps she would have told her a bit about the party while Nala plodded back into the basket and curled up with the satisfied sigh that meant the herd was gathered. She was only a dumb animal, but sometimes it felt as though, without realizing it, Elisabeth had robbed herself of the closest thing she had to a companion. Someone to share all the empty spaces with after Winter.

"So, let us raise our glasses to Elisabeth, whose brainchild Callocain we're so tremendously excited about," concluded Marcus, clinking his glass against hers. "Cheers!"

Applause broke out; some people even whooped, and one of the secretaries stepped forward to take a picture. It had been years since Danish Pharma had patented a brand-new formula. And this time it wasn't just another middle-of-the-road antidepressant or yet one more anti-anxiety med that worked about as well as all the rest: no, this was an entirely new creation. A landslide victory. Even though Marcus would end up with most of the glory, at least as far as the outside world was concerned, Callocain was first and foremost Elisabeth's achievement, and everybody in the garden knew it.

She thanked every single member of her team by name with studied humility, giving a brief account of the ups and downs of the last seven years, from dropped petri dishes to drowned mice and now, at last, to the mourners, who after many months of sorrow, could be brought back to life.

"You all know how much this project means to me. In fact, I'd go so far as to say that Callocain, this dream, is one of the only things that has kept me going since my son was taken so long before his time."

She paused a moment to let the full impact of the words sink in. The reality was that it had been a long time since she'd felt genuine emotion when talking about Winter. Words could lose their meaning, you could wear them out, and just then, already half-playing someone else, she felt nothing at all.

"I'd like to give a big thanks to all of you who believed in the idea. I truly believe we're on the verge of a unique breakthrough. Which, after all, is the reason we all got into this business in the first place: to change people's lives for the better. Cheers!"

She took a step forward and raised her glass. Forced her face into the right folds, just as she had forced her life into a pattern that made it possible to go on, cleansed of dog hair, childish laughter, and a warm body to hold close at night.

CHAPTER TWELVE

October 2024

———

THORSTEN

IT'S PACKED SOLID WHEN THORSTEN, out of breath, steps into the auditorium. He'd spent so much time puzzling about Callocain that he would have forgotten his lecture that day if a notification from his calendar hadn't given him a nudge.

"My apologies," he mumbles, fiddling with his computer. The topic that day is intervention, with a special focus on the therapeutic alliance, and he knows the material back to front. Yet, more than once, he mixes up key terms.

"No, not transference," he interrupts himself, "I mean, of course..." He turns and stares up at the screen, where the letters are huge and fuzzy. What was he about to say? "Just a sec."

The typing hands freeze. The clatter of many keyboards dies away, and one by one his students lift their heads from their open screens, until every eye in the hall is fixed on him. The gulf is abruptly insurmountable—right now it's easy to forget that he was once exactly like them. That they are on the same side. The button-hole microphone casts his echoing breath through the speakers; the whole auditorium is waiting for him, and he's saying nothing. Then a hand is raised.

"You were telling us about setting," says a dark-haired woman. Thorsten knows her well: she always sits in the front row, she's a little older than the average student, and she's one of the few who has the guts to stick her neck out. "You were saying it's important to establish a framework early on, so you can return to it later if the client challenges it. Right?"

Thorsten stares out over the army of people. He tries to screw his head back on straight, but he can't think straight; it's all slipping away.

"We're going to take a break." He blinks hard. "Then we'll pick up after that. Fifteen minutes."

An uneasy murmur drifts toward the ceiling as the students bump their way out through the rows of chairs.

Somehow he makes it through the second half, and as soon as the last images appear onscreen, he thanks the students for their time and scurries out of the auditorium before anyone can accost him. He needs a quiet minute to collect himself, but back at his office he stops short just inside the doorway. His computer is on. Warily, he looks around. Hudson is glowering down at him from his portrait hanging on the wall; there's no answer to be found there, but something must have happened while he was gone. It's been two hours since he left, and he locked both his computer and his door, didn't he? Even if he didn't, the screen should have gone to sleep ages ago.

He goes tentatively back out into the empty corridor, peering to one side, then the next. But, really, what is he thinking? That one of his colleagues came in and ransacked his computer while he was out? It sounds nuts. What would they even be looking for? In a daze he crosses over to his desk and sinks into his chair. Maybe they were right after all, Kamilla with her paper-thin solicitude and Svend, whom he hasn't spoken to since their little tiff in Miguel's office. Maybe he really is losing his grip.

SHADI

ALTHOUGH SHADI CAN SEE ANNA has added some notes to the shared folder from her visit to Danish Pharma, as well as a new chunk of text about the grief test, she once again opens SPSS. She promised Thorsten she'd give it one more shot, and she's decided to focus on empathy. First, she asks the program to plot the development of the entire group of 398 grief patients over time, from the first test to the last. It presents the information as two columns, one of which is marginally lower than the other. Fine. This means the participants underwent a slight drop during the six-month project, which accords with Anton's results. In his summary, she reads that the control group scored roughly the same throughout, while those on medication saw, on average, a modest drop. But Anton's approach, comparing the averages of the two groups, means that the results don't say much about what's happening at the extremes. Especially given that he's removed his three "outliers."

She drums on the edge of the table, wondering why on earth Anton went about it like that. After all, you could easily imagine a situation in which the participants reacted wildly differently: where some of them experienced a decrease in empathy and others an increase, while still others stayed the same, and all that variation is glossed over if you approach things in the way Anton has done.

Outside it's raining. Fat droplets that tap against the windowpane like insects in the summer, while Shadi's hands move across the keyboard at ever-increasing speed. There must be a way in. Even if she can't separate the participants on Callocain from the placebo group, it must still be possible to ask the question she can't find anywhere in Anton's documents. Namely, whether there is a connection between the patients' mental state and their ability to put themselves in others' shoes. Between their grief score and empathy.

She unticks the necessary boxes, asks for a calculation, and hits Enter. Gazes at the screen unblinking. And there, as if by magic, the material opens up.

It's stopped raining. The city's face transforms as lights are switched on in apartments all around, but Shadi is so engrossed she barely notices. The diagram that has been drawn before her eyes looks like sauce spattered across a white wall. Empathy scores along the vertical axis, grief along the horizontal. The correlation is a slope from the top left corner toward the bottom right; SPSS has even drawn a line through the 398 dots to make things still clearer. There is a connection, as expected. Time now for the real question: Does the use of Callocain affect this connection, and if so, how?

Hastily she finds two of the articles she printed last time she was at the university. Since AU is the only place in the world, apart from Danish Pharma, that is allowed to conduct trials with Callocain yet, she has no other results to compare directly. But the two articles she's holding examined the degree of empathy shown by the bereaved, just without medication involved, and they used the same kind of scatter diagram as the one Shadi has just conjured onto her own screen. The difference is striking once you know where to look. The diagonal cloud of dots is more con-densed in the two foreign charts, which tells her that the correla-tion between grief and empathy was stronger in their studies. Her pulse thuds against her skin; something *is* different in AU's trial, then. Using Callocain does affect the relationship between grief and empathy, although at first glance she can't tell how. There's also one more difference, at least, between her diagram and theirs, which is what's happening in the bottom left-hand corner. This is where Mikkel and presumably the two other outliers are located, and where a low grief score and low empathy meet. Shadi enlarges the image. She zooms in on the anchorless points in her diagram. The plots in the other two studies don't look like this—their lower left corners are all but empty. She zooms in again. Something tells her it's here, in this very corner, that the answer to Thorsten's question will be found.

THORSTEN

THE SOUNDS OF "SO WHAT" are floating through the living room. *Kind of Blue* is the record Thorsten always returns to when he needs to steady himself. In fact, this is his second copy; the first he wore out in the months after Anita left for Åbyhøj with Andreas. Sometimes, steadying yourself takes time.

He shuts his eyes. Pushes aside the image of that ominously glowing screen in his office, the sense of being busy yet unable to move a muscle. He'll have to trust that Shadi would call with good news tomorrow, because there's nothing he can do right now anyway. Instead, he concentrates on the music, following one instrument at a time—piano, bass, the distinctive trumpet—but the exercise doesn't have its usual meditative effect. Something is keeping him stuck, a flutter in his chest, like when you're walking down an alley in the dark and sense someone behind you. Like you should turn around before it's too late.

He's awoken by a loud noise, as though something has been flung against the window. The record has reached "All Blues" now, so he must have nodded off, but he's ninety per cent sure the sound came from the real world. He gets to his feet in a muddle and examines the east-facing windows, where there's nothing to be seen, then the ones looking south. It's hard to make out, what with the reflection of the lamps in the room and the black garden outside, but there's something there, isn't there? A greasy smear, obstructing his view of the apple tree? The glass is smooth and cool against his fingertips. When he opens the window, his attention is grabbed by something moving, almost alive, stuck in the dark blotch on the glass. Feathers.

But even after it occurs to him to use the flashlight on his phone, when he sees it's only a streak of blood and a couple of dark, bedraggled feathers and realizes what has happened, he isn't reassured. The sudden jolt awake and the menacing thud have got under his skin, and although it feels stupid to admit it, he has to force himself to put his jacket on and go outside.

The house is built on a slope, so that there's a drop of nearly six metres outside the living room, and he finds the black mass underneath the windows, right by the door to the basement. He looks around the garden. On the other side of the hedge is the neighbour's plot, but it's half past ten and no one's out this late. There's no sign of anything out of the ordinary. Cautiously, he picks up what he recognizes is a blackbird. It droops lifelessly in his hands. Their skeletons are hollow, he remembers, yet he's taken aback by its lightness. He strokes a finger gingerly along the glossy feathers of its wing, as a gust of wind sends a shiver through him. Its neck must be broken, and although he knows the thought is absurd, it takes shape nonetheless: that someone broke the creature's neck on purpose, well before it hit his window. That this—this is a warning.

ANNA

"REMEMBER WHEN MOM TRIED TO get you to play badminton?" Her dad is holding one of her mother's old trophies. His beard is shorter than last time, almost clean-shaven, and his shirt front is dotted with purple splotches of what looks like the beetroot he ate for lunch. "You had so much pent-up energy, and you refused to put up with the serving and picking up shuttlecocks and all that."

It's the night of Maiken's party, and Anna really ought to be in town by now, hunting for a present. Instead she's here, sitting on the parquet with her dad. They've opened the big cupboard on the far wall, and Anna is sorting, making a virtue of looking at every single thing she takes out as exactly that, a thing. Not her mom's treasured possessions, each with a memory like a halo in the light of the standing lamp—just objects you could use or throw away.

"It was so slow-paced," she says. "I never got why Mom was so into it. And then that smell that was in the hall—what was that?"

"Sweat, I suppose."

She wrinkles her nose. He's probably right, but it was more than that, it was wood and plastic and years of poor ventilation, and she never got used to it.

"What about this?" She points at the sewing machine. It's never far away, the sound of the needle bobbing up and down as her mother depressed the pedal, the sight of her guiding the fabric through the machine with pins in the corner of her mouth and the measuring tape like a yellow snake around her neck. "That stuff's just gathering dust, isn't it?"

But her dad doesn't reply. He's still holding the trophy from the club championship in 1994, rubbing his finger back and forth over the engraving. His head is bowed.

"I'll put it in the box to get rid of," Anna decides, and puts the heavy machine next to some dishes and a stack of tops that smell like Mom. There's nothing here she wants to keep, and she won't use it anyway. She's got enough. The specially chosen things her mom gave her with feverish hands when it was clear she wasn't getting better: a sort of diary about Anna as a child, full of pictures she'd never seen before, and the sweater she had knitted while expecting. Anna wore it for weeks afterward, although the wool was scratchy at the wrists. It was like a spell. *If I'm wearing the top, Mom can't die.*

Later, a couple of weeks after the funeral, she had taken some more clothes, and a necklace and the perfume that her mom had always worn, until the day she couldn't bear any scents at all, not even laundry soap, not even the food others cooked for her.

"Anyway." Anna wipes her nose with the back of her hand. "I guess that's going too?" She reaches for the trophy, and her dad lifts his twisted face toward her. "What?" she asks, biting her cheek so hard it splits.

He shakes his head. "I can't."

She wonders whether she could take something else from the cupboard instead, ask about something practical to jolt them out of the moment, but it's too late. He genuinely can't. And maybe that's fair enough. Her parents had a life together she knows nothing of—they were something before her and something after. The day they told her about the leukemia, they had carefully pre-pared everything. Gone to the doctor and the hospital about the wound that wouldn't heal, the blood that wouldn't run clean, the fear that seeped down into the sheets. Anna was their third wheel, the one they told together that Mom was sick, and when she left them again that night, she couldn't know how they stayed behind, whether they let something drop. You don't know everything. And that night she understood for the first time that her parents shared a closeness she could never fully enter.

"It doesn't matter, Dad," she says, wishing she meant it. "We'll just wait. There's plenty of time."

SHADI

SHADI HATES SPEAKING ON THE phone, but when she calls Thorsten that afternoon, she's even more nervous than normal. Or maybe *nervous* isn't the right word. She just hopes he can use what she's now spent nearly twenty-four hours piecing together.

"Tell me what you've got," he says. "It sounds like Kamilla is sending out the press release tomorrow, so this is our last chance."

"Sure," she says, and clears her throat. It occurs to her that this is the first time today she's used her voice. She's been sitting in front of the computer since she got up. "I'm still not sure—it's not easy without the code. For example, I can show that some of the participants have improved, but I don't know if they're on the medication or not, and it's the same for empathy. But then I tried looking at the connection between the grief and empathy scores across the entire group."

"Okay," he says. "And...?"

"And I found a negative correlation of minus 0.6." The words are shiny and clean, slipping so easy off the tongue. "In the other couple of studies I found on grief and empathy, it's around minus 0.8."

"Without medication?"

"Exactly."

She can almost hear his brain working to get the numbers to make sense.

"So if we assume that the ones who felt better are the ones who were given Callocain, then those are also the ones who experienced this more marked drop in empathy?" he says slowly. "Is that right?"

"Maybe." How is she supposed to explain it to him when she isn't even sure herself? "I think there's a lot of variation in what occurs. Some patients experience a slight decrease in empathy, and stay at that level even after they're feeling better. Others go back to normal, or even higher. And then there are a few special cases, including the three Anton removed. They're obviously feeling better, even though their empathy scores have nosedived."

Although she stumbles over a few words, Shadi forces herself to keep going. "I think Anton is right that the average drop is minimal, especially without the outliers, but that glosses over some major fluctuations. Plus, it's pretty much just one part of the test that saw a shift, so that makes the overall drop in empathy look even smaller. If you just look at that one part in isolation, the numbers are even crazier."

"Which part is that?" asks Thorsten.

"The one called compassion something or other."

A murmur from Thorsten. "Interesting."

She's pretty sure she knows what he means, but she asks anyway.

"Well, that particular combination—that the score in one area remains more or less constant while the other drops—only makes the whole scenario even more unpleasant," he explains. "Because that would mean these individuals know that the people around them are thinking and feeling differently from themselves. They have no trouble reading facial expressions or body language, and they understand, for instance, when someone is scared or upset. They just don't care anymore."

The autism test and the psychopath test. That was how the two were described in a critical blog post Shadi had come across earlier when she was hunting for background information on the empathy test. In the research group's own material, it stated that while one part of the test evaluated an individual's ability to read other people's mental states, the other spoke to how those states affected them.

"It would be a tremendous help if we could go through your calculations together," says Thorsten. "And in any case, I don't have the program you're using. Would you mind coming to my office tomorrow morning? Say, eight? Then I'll take everything to Kamilla after that."

"Of course," replies Shadi. It's wild to think that her calculations might be used to convince Thorsten's boss.

"But the meeting itself I'll have to do alone," he says. "I'm not sure what Kamilla would say to the idea of a student as a statistics consultant, and I've probably already got you far more mixed up in all this than I should."

She hasn't thought much about that until now, but of course he's right. Thorsten sent her someone else's data without their consent or any type of security, and although she's taken good care of the material, it's unlikely to go over well with the boss. "But, Thorsten?"

"Yes?"

"What does this mean?"

There's silence on the line, and Shadi pictures him. Maybe he's scratching his neck, in the frantic way she's seen him do in lectures when he's frustrated with something.

"As far as I can see, it means one of two things," he says at last. "Either a mistake has been made somewhere along the line, probably by Anton. AU is a serious university with a lot of top-notch researchers, and if you'd asked me before all this whether any of us might get up to anything ill-informed or even deceitful, I'd have thought you were joking."

"Or?"

"Yes," he sighs. "The other possibility, which sadly I'm increasingly inclined to believe, is that someone saw the same alterations in empathy as we did. And that for some reason he or she has manipulated the data to hide them."

August 2022
———

ELISABETH

ALTHOUGH ELISABETH WAS LESS BUSY now than before, she still went into the office on the weekends. Letting herself into the vast, sacred space, she felt a rush of mercurial freedom. Other times she worked from home, but even after all these years she risked falling into reveries, thinking of another kind of Saturday, one where the dog barked in the garden above Winter's merry shrieks, or of waiting while he was in hospital, of the way his toys crouched in their baskets as though ready to spring.

It was one such Saturday, in the middle of the fiercest heat-wave of the year, when she'd gone in to check through some papers, that Kamilla rang. They had known each other for several years and had developed a kind of unspoken alliance—two determined, ambitious women in a world still dominated even now by white, tie-wearing men. If an especially persistent investigator started digging into the donations Danish Pharma's foundation gave at intervals to the university, they might discover a pattern, but nothing could be proved, and that was the crucial thing.

"We've got a project on the go here I think might interest you," said Kamilla. "A study into how your new wonder drug works."

"Callocain? I can explain that to you right now." Elisabeth tried to keep her voice calm, although all her senses were alert. "But something tells me it's not proteins and neurotransmitters you want to know about."

Kamilla was quick to laugh, at least when there was money on the line. "It was your boss, actually, who suggested it the other day," she said. "A one-off agreement in which AU is allowed to study the drug right up until it hits the market."

"Marcus? What's he getting out of it?"

"Momentum," Kamilla answered dryly. "If it goes well, that is. In the media, maybe even in the wider public. A drug to treat grief is a tricky thing—could be a tough sell. Much easier if a group of the country's leading scientists vouch for it."

She continued talking about the study, which was due to start the following year, if all went according to plan. Elisabeth was half-listening, trying to work out the best approach. Letting an independent body study Callocain before the pills were even ready for sale sounded to her mind like an unnecessarily big gamble. Marcus must really believe in Callocain if he was even considering it.

"We'll be seeking funding from the Independent Research Fund," Kamilla concluded, "so it's more the next projects I'm worried about. In the end it's all a question of resources, you know."

"Then it's lucky we've got a meeting with the foundation coming up," Elisabeth replied. "I'll be sure to put in a good word for your department. And, as it happens, I know a great statistician you should really bring on board for your grief project. Anton Maninnen—one of the best there is."

She had to think quickly now. Ever since autumn 2019 she'd had a hold on Anton, a former statistician at Danish Pharma: by a stroke of luck she'd caught him in a rather unsavoury exchange, selling health information belonging to unwitting trial participants, which was being used to tailor advertising on Facebook. Instead of exposing him she had decided to keep him in reserve, waiting for the moment when she could use the knowledge to her best advantage—and this could very well be it.

"Actually, we've already got an excellent statistician," Kamilla began, but Elisabeth cut her off.

"No," she said. "It has to be Anton, or you'll need to look elsewhere for funding from now on."

Kamilla was quiet for a second or two, then she laughed again. "Of course," she said. "Then that's what we'll do."

"Good." Elisabeth had stood up and begun to pace back and forth between the wall and the desk. "I'll send you his details. It would be nice to get him involved in a few other projects as well, and preferably as soon as possible. Is there anything else I should be aware of?"

"I don't think so," said Kamilla. "Except maybe Thorsten Gjeldsted, one of our psychology professors. He's all right really, but he has a tendency to sink his teeth into the tiniest details and bite down until they cut right through. That's assuming there's something to bite into, of course."

Elisabeth assured her this was not the case, and she meant it. Since the trouble with the disturbed mice, there had been no further issues with Callocain. Danish Pharma's various studies had revealed no side effects other than nausea, difficulty falling asleep, and a few similarly predictable nuisances, and Elisabeth genuinely believed there was nothing else to find. So it irritated her enormously that Kamilla's project was about to breathe life back into her old nightmare: that despite her best efforts, something would bring down the whole edifice she had fought so hard to build.

CHAPTER THIRTEEN

October 2024

———

ANNA

"THERE'S A TEXT FROM YOUR dissertation buddy," Siri calls from inside the living room. Anna pulls a face. The headache that was creeping up on her at her father's house earlier is now gnawing its way through her skull. She quickly takes an aspirin and goes into the living room, replies to Shadi, and tosses her phone back onto the table.

"What did she want?"

Anna slumps down next to Siri on the sofa, so that they're lying with their heads at opposite ends. There's a flickering behind her eyes, and when she closes them the whole room spins.

"Oh, it's just Thorsten and his project," she says. "Apparently Shadi's got a meeting with him tomorrow morning to go through her calculations. See if they're reliable."

"If what are reliable?" Siri asks, but Anna shrugs and turns her attention to the television. She doesn't feel like talking about the dissertation or statistics or anything remotely to do with psychology right now. Siri nudges her with her foot.

"Something about how Callocain might have side effects we didn't know about," she mumbles. "It's a pretty big deal, if it's true, and she asked if I wanted to come to the meeting. Shall we watch something else...or?"

All she wants to do is lie here and cuddle up with Siri until the headache goes away, to forget that there exists a world outside, and that pretty soon she'll have to get ready if she doesn't want to miss Maiken's birthday party. But, abruptly, Siri is in the hall.

"I've just got to make a phone call," she shouts. "Will you let me back in again in a minute?"

Anna stands by the window with her thighs pressed against the grooves of the radiator, watching as Siri leaves through the front door. Of course, everyone's boundaries are different when it comes to privacy, but it's starting to bother her that Siri is so secretive. The party tonight would be the perfect opportunity to share a bit more of their lives with each other, but Siri insists she's got an important presentation on Monday, so she has to go home and work. How is Anna supposed to take that? Apart from their very first date, they've only ever hung out at her place. She knows nothing about Siri's house except that it's somewhere in Risskov. Now she's wandering around downstairs in her silk-lined coat, which probably cost about the same as Anna's yearly student grant, talking to someone about something Anna must not under any circumstances be allowed to hear.

"What was so important?" she asks when Siri comes back. She's skipped the shower and is hurriedly putting on some makeup.

"Just a work thing," Siri answers lightly, and lies down on the bed in a last fan-shaped ray of evening sun. She turns her face toward the window and shuts her eyes.

"Always so mysterious," says Anna. And then, before she can think better of it, "We haven't been over to your place yet. Are you living with someone, is that it?"

The question reverberates between them. Anna waits, lipstick raised, suddenly afraid that Siri will be angry with her or, worse, that she will laugh and ask, *What did you expect? What do you think this is?*

"I've never lived with a partner, if that's what you mean," says Siri. "But someone did live there once."

Immediately Anna is almost hyperfocused, Siri's pine-needle scent prickling in her nose.

"Who?"

"My son." Siri's voice is so low now that Anna has to hold her breath to hear her. "I'll tell you about him one day, I promise."

Although Siri doesn't say so directly, Anna's in no doubt about what she means, and it's as though something she has always recognized in Siri suddenly takes shape right there in the bedroom.

"Maybe I should cancel?" she asks, going over to the bed and taking Siri's hand. "So we can just stay here?"

But Siri shakes her head. "I'm okay," she says. "It's a long time ago, all that. Off you go." She lets Anna give her a single kiss before pushing her away. "We'll see each other soon, all right?"

A few hours later, Anna is struggling to keep her balance as she squats over the piss-spattered toilet at the club. She lifts her head and tries to focus on Maiken.

"I'd have really loved for you to meet Siri," she says, pulling her pants back up with some difficulty. "I'm sure you'd like her."

"I know that, sweetheart." Maiken reaches out and strokes her hair. She's faintly cross-eyed, as she always is when she's been drinking, and the curly streamers Anna has pinned into her bun are hanging down over her shoulder. "Next time, eh? Come on, let's dance."

And they do. At first Anna checks her phone every time she goes to the bar. It feels wrong to be apart from Siri so soon after learning she'd once lost a child. She was really kind to Anna the day she told her about her mom. But Siri isn't answering her texts, so eventually Anna leaves her phone in her bag. Standing in the middle of the dance floor, she stretches up toward the flashing lights and the rhythm that comes crashing at her. She's finally getting drunk enough to forget, drunk enough that it feels like anything might happen. As though anyone could give her something and take it back again, lick the dampness from her skin and push through her without it meaning the slightest little thing at all.

THORSTEN

AT FIRST, THORSTEN CAN'T MAKE heads or tails of it when he looks at the clock radio and sees the time is eighteen minutes past two. He rubs his eyes, but the numbers are the same, and through a veil of sleep he tries to work out what's going on. The room is dark, apart from the window's slightly paler rectangle. It must be the rattling, buzzing sound coming from the phone that woke him. The voice on the line is gravelly when he picks up.

"Thorsten? What's happening to me?"

"Sorry." Thorsten, dazed, pushes himself up into a sitting position. "Who am I speaking to?"

"I hit a guy over the head with a bottle! He went out like a light."

He recognizes the voice. "Is that you, Mikkel? Tell me where you are, I'll call an ambulance," he says, but Mikkel replies that that's not why he's calling.

"There were people everywhere, so someone must have done that," he says. "I just want to know what's in those pills you're giving me. That bottle smashed to pieces in my hand—I had no idea it was possible to bleed so much. And you know what the worst thing is?"

"No?" Thorsten waits for him to go on, heart sinking.

"I could have kept going." Mikkel's voice is rising. "If that bottle hadn't broken, I would have kept hitting! That's not fucking normal!"

There's a plaintive note somewhere underneath the anger, and although what Mikkel's saying is awful, Thorsten almost feels sorry for him. This young man who, on a perfectly normal Wednesday, lost both the woman he loved and their child. Who now, after taking part in Thorsten's grief project, seems to be incapable of feeling either the pain of his loss or the horror of injuring another human being. But is it Mikkel's fault? Surely this is exactly the sort of thing that gets taken into account by the courts—there's that paragraph about temporary insanity at the time of the offence. Is Mikkel in his right mind while he's on those pills? Is anybody?

"Look, we don't know if you've been getting calcium or the medication," he says, and tries to make his voice as soothing as possible. "So it's hard to say whether your fight has anything to do with the trial."

"What do you think?" Mikkel raises his voice again. "I could barely stand upright the first time I met you, I was so devastated— of course I've been getting the real pills. And now I'd like to know what the hell you've been giving me!"

Thorsten hesitates. He isn't sure how much he's allowed to share.

"There must be something! Why else would you ask all those questions every time I saw you?" Mikkel continues. "Asking me what I think other people are feeling, and when's the last time I did something to make someone else happy, all that stuff?"

And then Thorsten makes a decision. Who is he really protecting here? He's the one who has to live with this, and right now, frankly, there are bigger things at stake than confidentiality and research ethics. "It looks like Callocain might lead to some sort of reduced sensitivity toward other people," he says.

"Reduced sensitivity? You mean you stop caring?"

"Yes, you could put it like that."

There's silence at the other end.

"Listen, Mikkel. If I were you, I'd see I got rid of those pills as soon as possible."

No response.

"Are you listening, Mikkel? Right now."

"I don't understand how this could happen," Mikkel murmurs. "This isn't who I am at all."

SHADI

SHADI IS SITTING IN THE front room, lights off and the sea like a darker field behind her in the night, still too agitated to sleep. Her head is spinning with graphs and scattered figures. In a few hours she'll head over to the department to show Thorsten her calculations, and she wishes just a fraction of the peace she associates with water would rub off on her now. Her mom called earlier that evening, but instead of picking up she flipped her phone over. That conversation's too much for her right now. She won't tell her parents she and Emil are having problems until she knows what's going to happen herself.

If he were here, Emil would hold her and say something comforting, and after a few minutes it would become easier to breathe. But there's only her now, and she wraps the blanket more tightly around herself, reaching for her phone so she can think about something else. Anton Manninen, that's the name of the statistician whose footsteps she's spent a week retracing. It's like she knows him, through his tests and the way he writes, but when he appears onscreen, he looks nothing like what she'd imagined. A man almost transparent, with fine, whitish hair in a messy ring around his bald spot. He's been involved with the university for just under two years, but Shadi can't find his CV on the website, and there's no way to see what he studied. The eternal vagrant, drifting from one project to the next, always the expert, never a full-fledged member of the group. How does somebody end up like that? And if he really is the one who tampered with the numbers in the grief trial, as she's beginning to believe he is, then why did he do it?

Without dwelling on it too much, she realizes her heart rate has slowed. The distraction worked. Yawning, she's about to get up and go to bed when an image at the very bottom of the search results catches her eye. She clicks on it to get a better look at the slightly pixelated faces. It looks like some sort of party, outdoors, and the photographer has focused on a beautiful couple in the middle, a man in a suit and a woman in a red dress, clinking glasses. But that's

Anton in the corner, isn't it, champagne raised and hair practically radiant in the sun? She frowns, rereads the caption, and types four words into the search bar: Anton Maninnen, Danish Pharma.

THORSTEN

THORSTEN HAS JUST ARRIVED, STILL groggy after Mikkel's phone call in the middle of the night, when there's a knock at his office door. His first thought is that it must be Shadi, even more punctual than usual, but when he looks up, it's Anton in the doorway.

"Am I interrupting?"

"No, no." Thorsten waves him in, and the statistician holds out one of the hideous university-branded mugs they were given at the seminar last winter.

"Coffee? It's the good stuff from the third floor."

Thorsten accepts, still not sure what to make of the unexpected visit.

"I thought I'd just have a word with you about the project, if you've got time." Anton sits down. "It seemed like you had more questions than you were able to ask at the meeting."

"That's kind of you."

Thorsten clears his throat. There's a frog in it, and he takes another sip to wash it away. What's the best way to tackle this conversation? On an impulse he decides to show as many of his cards as possible, see what that does.

"In a nutshell, I'm wondering whether the average you've calculated is actually the best measure of empathy," he begins. "There seems to be a correlation between the participants who experienced a big improvement and the ones who showed the biggest drop in empathy, and that kind of thing can get lost if you take the approach that you did, can't it? Especially since you decided to remove three of the worst cases from the equation."

Anton scratches something on his cheek. His skin is red and rough, as though he's had a bad shave. "I didn't realize you were interested in statistics."

Thorsten shakes his head but is immediately seized by a violent fit of coughing. His entire throat is tickling. "Only on an amateur level," he manages to croak out when the coughing subsides.

"But you didn't find there was a correlation? Between clinical improvement and a drop in empathy among the subjects in active treatment?"

"I didn't, no, but it's an intriguing thought."

Anton is nodding to himself, and for a moment Thorsten almost thinks he might have misjudged him. That he should have gone to him directly straight away: a colleague who is every bit as nerdy about the science as he is, and who shares his vision that research should reflect reality as much as possible. But then a thin line slices down between Anton's nearly invisible brows.

"I'm just struggling to see the relevance for this particular study, since—as I've said several times—there is no actual decrease in empathy, it's simply that the status quo is maintained," he says. "It stagnates, but in all likelihood, it will eventually normalize, just like the others in the group agreed it would. If it will reassure you, I can take another look at the numbers, of course, but I think you're seeing things that aren't there."

Seeing things. Thorsten undoes the top button of his shirt. That was probably what Svend meant when he said he'd gone off the deep end. Kamilla, Miguel, all the clever people around him seem to think he's on the wrong track. Then again, they haven't seen all the evidence he has slowly gathered, and he's looking forward to getting it out in the open, no matter the consequences. Make-or-break time. He gets up to open the window, let in some fresh air, but stops short. There's a lurching sensation in his legs.

"That's funny," he says, "it feels like…"

But he can't get another word out before he's launched into another coughing fit. The tickle is uncontrollable now, reminding him unmistakably of the time he was stung by a bee at his aunt's birthday party, or the time there were traces of nuts in the shop-bought cake, even though the ingredients said otherwise. His throat clenches into a rough, obstinate fist as panic rises. And Anton, can't he see Thorsten needs help? He's just sitting there, pale eyes staring.

He needs to find his EpiPen. Thorsten takes a step toward his bag but trips and falls, landing outstretched on the floor. Out of the corner of his eye he registers that Anton is finally on his feet.

"Help," he whispers through the unbearable pressure in his throat. "My bag, can you…"

But that's as far as he gets before the coughing takes him.

September 2024

—

ELISABETH

ELISABETH SPENT THE GAP BETWEEN the morning meeting with Kamilla and her final contribution to the grief project a few hours afterwards in one of the university's spare offices. The laptop was open in front of her. There was plenty of work to be getting on with, but instead she had turned toward the yellowing park outside the window. She couldn't stop wondering whether Winter might have applied here, when the time came—whether his enthusiasm for drawing would have developed into a career as a designer, or if the way he had soaked up every word, enchanted, as she read to him out loud meant he'd have become the kind of person who lived through language.

But, as always when she got carried away, the daydream shattered far too quickly. No matter what she did to project him into the future, Winter never grew any older than five. Even now, as she tried forcibly to barge him into the group of young people walking down the path, he remained a little boy with a voice far too light and eyes that believed anything was possible.

She sighed and turned away again. At that moment the door to Thorsten's office opened on the other side of the corridor, and from where she was sitting, she could observe him and the young woman he'd been talking to for the past thirty minutes. It looked like she'd been crying. Something about her glinting eyelashes and the way she moved, like a predator that might at any moment spring, drew Elisabeth to her feet. Without really wanting to she had overheard parts of their conversation, since at several points it had grown quite loud, and now she watched the mismatched couple as they walked along the hall. The student, still frantically chattering about the thesis she was so desperate to write, and Thorsten, the psychology professor Kamilla had warned her about on the phone, back before the project had even been launched. The one with a tendency to sink his teeth in. So far, he hadn't seemed particularly intimidating, least of all right now, with his too-short trousers and incipient bald spot, as he listened to the agitated young woman by his side. But Anton had warned Elisabeth that there might be some issues with the results, so she had to be extra-vigilant. And maybe, she thought as she unlocked her phone, still not taking her eyes off the two people in the corridor, maybe it would turn out once again that whoever bit first would get the last laugh.

CHAPTER FOURTEEN

October 2024

SHADI

AFTERWARDS, SHADI THINKS IT MUST have been a sort of half-choked rattling noise that made her turn the handle and open the door instead of waiting in the hall. Thorsten is lying on the carpet. He stares up at her with wild eyes, sounds pitching clumsily out of his mouth, incoherent, and as he lies there, he reminds her of something inside herself. The fear of going mad, perhaps, of letting all things slide. Someone has electrocuted him, she thinks in bewilderment; it looks like an invisible hand is trying to shake a secret out of him.

"Tsss." He spits onto the floor, breath drawn in thin, squealing heaves.

Shadi follows his gaze and sees his bag over by the shelf.

"Tssss," he hisses again, and at last she reacts.

She hears herself shouting for help in a loud, frightened voice. Maybe this is like that time at primary school, when Sanne had a seizure in the middle of PE and bit off the tip of her own tongue. What's she supposed to do now—keep his head safe, put something in his mouth? She opens Thorsten's bag with feverish hands, rooting through the compartments at random, and there—that must be it, a yellow box containing something that looks like two marker pens.

Somehow she gets the syringes unwrapped, but her hands are shaking so much she almost drops them. Thorsten is gasping for air, beet-red in the face, but Shadi can't bring herself to inject him. She knows it's what she has to do, but getting her body to respond is impossible. Thorsten is going to die, because she doesn't have what it takes to save him.

At that moment, there are running footsteps in the corridor.

"Have you called for help?" shouts a woman who must be a department secretary, putting her face so close that her menthol breath makes Shadi blink. "Hello, have you called an ambulance?"

"Here," Shadi hands her the syringes. "I can't."

After she's told the paramedics what she knows and Thorsten has been driven away, Shadi goes into the washroom. Her trembling fingers automatically look up Emil's number on her phone, then dismiss it again. Instead she stands in front of the mirror, washes her hands for a long time, and splashes her face with cold water. Imagine if he didn't survive.

The first person she sees when she steps back out into the hall is Anna.

"Shadi! Did I miss the meeting?" Anna is walking toward her. When she's close enough to see her face properly, she exclaims, "Are you okay?"

"Thorsten has just been taken away in an ambulance," says Shadi. "It was me who found him."

"You're not serious?"

"He was lying on the floor when I came in."

"No way." Anna's eyes are huge. "What's wrong with him?"

"I don't know." Shadi shakes her head. "It looked like epilepsy or something."

"Jesus." Anna takes a step to one side, as though someone has knocked her off course, but then turns toward Shadi again. "Come on," she says. "We're going to the café, and you're going to tell me everything."

ANNA

"IMAGINE IF HE NEVER WOKE up, or he's brain-damaged because I couldn't make myself inject him. I completely froze up, you know what I mean?"

Shadi's pupils are twice the size they normally are—she looks almost high. Anna nods, although the truth is that paralysis isn't in her nature. She's more the inject-first-and-ask-questions-later type.

"I'll just call and find out how he's doing," she says. "And you shouldn't think like that. Who knows what would have happened if you hadn't gotten there early."

They've ended up in the library garden, and Anna finds a quiet nook to make the call. The air feels dense and clammy, and her heart is pounding. She got home at five this morning from Maiken's party, but right now she doesn't feel the tiredness at all.

"Yeah, hi, I'm Thorsten Gjeldsted's daughter, he's just been admitted," she says when she's been put through to a nurse in intensive care.

With a little coaxing she gets the woman at the other end to tell her that Thorsten went into cardiac arrest following what appears to be anaphylactic shock, and that his condition is critical but stable. They're confident, says the nurse, and when she repeats that everything will be fine, tears well up in Anna's eyes. Cardiac arrest. Another body in a white bed.

"So, he'll make it?" she asks. "You're sure he'll make it?"

When the conversation is over, she stands there for a minute. The high-ceilinged, plant-filled room is like a damp terrarium around her. She takes a few deep breaths and goes back to Shadi.

"So?"

"Sounds like it was touch and go," she begins, but stops herself when she sees Shadi clasp her hands in front of her mouth in a pleading gesture. "But look, don't worry, he's okay now. He's fine."

"Oh, thank God." Shadi exhales audibly. "Do they know what happened?"

Anna shakes her head. Thorsten's lifeless body in the hospital bed, the billowing curtain Anna always drew before she sat down. Her mother's warm, dry hands.

"The nurse said it was an allergic reaction. I mean, there are loads of things he can't have."

"Okay, but…" Shadi leans in and lowers her voice, as though about to share a secret. "Doesn't it seem like almost too much of a coincidence? Him having an attack like that, right before he's about to tell Kamilla what we found?"

Despite everything, Anna can't help but laugh. "Oh, come on," she protests, "don't you think maybe the guy just accidentally ate a nut?"

The idea that Thorsten's episode was the result of an assassination attempt is pretty far-fetched, but Shadi looks like she means it. She starts to explain what she and Thorsten have discovered over the past few days. A lot of it is quite technical, and Anna soon gives up on trying to follow everything. But there's something about a code Shadi's missing, some tests she ran anyway, and a way of slicing the data that makes it look like people on Callocain turn into psychopaths. At the last part, her eyes widen.

"Seriously?" she blurts out.

Shadi smiles sheepishly. "That might be a bit of an exaggeration, the psychopath stuff," she says, "but something does happen to empathy. Do you remember when we talked about mirror neurons in our cognition lectures?"

Anna nods. "How when I move, something in your brain reacts as though you'd done it yourself?"

"Exactly. And if I cry, your mirror neurons help you imagine what it would be like if it was you who was sad." Shadi shrugs. "I have no idea if that has anything to do with this, but it's as though Callocain makes something about that resonance between humans go haywire—it makes people care about each other less. Not all of them, I mean, probably only a few per cent are affected. But still."

"A few per cent adds up. More than 200,000 people are bereaved every year in Denmark, and if we say that fifteen per cent of them will be diagnosed with prolonged grief disorder, and even if just half of them take the medication…" Anna tries to work it out in her head, but Shadi is quicker.

"Then two per cent would be approximately three hundred people," she says.

"Three hundred," Anna repeats. She already finds that number terrifying. "And if we include the rest of Europe, plus obviously the USA further down the line, then we're talking about millions of people newly bereaved every year. There would be thousands of them who end up with these issues. Just think how many school shootings that could lead to."

Shadi practically begs Anna to come with her to see Kamilla, and although she'd rather visit Thorsten in the hospital, or maybe see about getting home and crawling into bed, she relents. They make it all the way to the front entrance before Shadi mentions the last part of her theory. That it's the statistician on the grief project who has manipulated the numbers, because he's in cahoots with Danish Pharma.

"I know how that sounds," she says, "but it's as though he used these particular calculations specifically to get the results he wanted. And think about this—I was googling him last night, and it's almost impossible to find anything about his past online, but then I stumbled across a picture from Danish Pharma's summer party in 2019. I'm almost sure it's him, just look at the hair."

She passes her phone to Anna, who dutifully looks first at the picture on the university's website, then at the one from the party.

"Yeah, it could definitely be him." She's about to hand the phone back when a figure catches her attention. The dark curls, the line of the throat. The way that all the eyes around her are somehow drawn in. "Who is that?"

There's a sharp jab in her chest. She enlarges the grainy image, but that only makes it harder to see anything at all.

"In the dress?" Shadi takes the phone back. "I think she's the one who invented Callocain. Elisabeth something."

Anna exhales the air she's evidently been holding; so it isn't her, after all. Of course it isn't.

"Wasn't she the one Thorsten said you should talk to when you went down there? The consultant? Here she is." This time the picture is pin-sharp and taken straight from Danish Pharma's website. "Elisabeth Siri Nordin."

CHAPTER FIFTEEN

October 2024

———

ELISABETH

ELISABETH IS CROUCHED IN FRONT of the patch of earth that is Winter's. She brushes away a few leaves and lays her hands on the rough stone. The sun has warmed it; it's a clear, crisp autumn day, the kind she loves. And then it occurs to her that she doesn't really feel anything. That perhaps she hasn't really felt much since those first appalling months when she was fighting not to tumble out through all the openings of herself. It's been a long time now. What is a person who doesn't feel things? She straightens up. Can losing a child be that devastating, can grief make a person blunt like that? Block all the entrances and exits like clinging mud that binds to the receptors and cuts you off from the outside world? Or is it just her, is it that she couldn't drag herself back out?

On her way through the cemetery, she nearly bumps into a tall man with sad eyes. He's new but comes here often. One day she walked past the gravestone he visits, and if the age is anything to go by, then it must be his wife, or maybe a sister, who has died. They exchange nods but never a word, although they share the heaviest weight of all. She hopes he gets more out of coming here than she does. Her visits to his grave rarely bring relief, and she doesn't believe that Winter is here more than anywhere else; the truth, probably, is that he's in her, always. Sometimes she thinks she mostly comes here to see if she can hurt herself. To lift the scab on the old wound, so that it will never be allowed to heal.

Not long afterwards, she's home. A warm light flows in through the windows in the living room. She should have sold this hunk of a house ages ago, really. There's something morbid about walking across the same floors where Winter learned to crawl. She can see them in all the rooms, him and Nala, but that's exactly why leaving would mean letting go of too much. Unbearable.

When the doorbell rings, she has no idea who it could be. There aren't many people in her life who would show up unannounced, and she's not expecting any guests. The floorboards are soft against her bare feet. If she tries, she can almost see Winter pull himself up using the banister and lurch toward her with outstretched arms. Then she opens the door.

"Hi, Elisabeth."

She ought to be flustered, embarrassed by the revelation, surely she should, but she can't help smiling. Maybe she can feel something after all. "Hi, Anna."

ANNA

SIRI, WHO APPARENTLY ALSO GOES by Elisabeth, doesn't look like someone who's just been unmasked. In fact, she looks genuinely sweet in her loose grey pantsuit, wearing an almost childlike smile, and for a moment Anna thinks she must have misunderstood. That the whole thing is a mistake, and Siri will turn out to have a twin who just happens to be a lead researcher at Danish Pharma.

But then Siri opens the door all the way and steps aside to make room.

"Hi, Anna," she says, and of course there is no one but her.

Anna walks past her into the large, beautiful house she'd been so excited to see, and nothing is as she had imagined.

"Would you like to come in?" Siri gestures with her hand, and Anna follows the movement with her eyes, down the hall and into the main room. It looks as though someone has stolen most of Siri's belongings, leaving her with only the bare essentials.

"Thanks," she says, and crosses her arms. "I'd just like to know why you lied to me."

"About the name, and...?" Siri tosses her hair. "You shouldn't read too much into it—that stuff doesn't really matter. I found out years ago how dearly people love to gossip if a woman allows herself an active dating life, so now I always do it this way. Lawyer for a night, you know."

She tousles her hair with her usual careless gesture and smiles at Anna, as though all is well now that they've got that little matter out of the way.

"What are you talking about?" Anna's nails are digging into the palms of her hands, but it's good, she needs it. "I was going to introduce you to my friends, if you'd bothered to come. I told you about my mother. Of course it matters!" She clasps her arms even more tightly across her chest. "And you weren't a lawyer for a night—try a month! Asking me questions about my thesis like you had no idea what any of it means, and you're the one who invented the pill I'm writing about!"

"You're right, that was stupid." Siri shakes her head. At least she's not smiling anymore. "I suppose I didn't think it would go this far, and somehow the time just passed. But I did think about us, actually," she says. "A lot. What kind of food I was going to make for you when you came to visit, how we'd read aloud to each other in the garden, all that stuff. We just live very different lives."

Anna stares at her. "Are you really that afraid of what people think?"

It must be the money Siri is talking about, the age difference and the silly hierarchy she's climbed. Apparently now that she's reached the top of it she has to change her name if she wants to have sex in peace. Is that really what all this is about?

But instead of answering, Siri holds out her hand. "Come on," she says, and takes a step toward the broad staircase. "There's something I would like to show you."

They're sitting on a child's bed almost identical to the one Anna slept in when she was little. Above them, a spaceship is dangling from a string attached to the ceiling. The room feels colder than the rest of the house, and the blue curtains are drawn. There's something about it that reminds her of her dad's apartment, and at first, she doesn't know what it is. Then it hits her: it's the same sense of time standing still.

"He's beautiful," she says, and he really is. Siri's son. There are pictures of him everywhere in here, but the two she likes best are hanging on the wall above the bed. She doesn't know much about children, but she'd put him at around four. His face is beaming, although his head seems a little big for his neck and slight shoulders. He looks like Siri.

"They were taken a few weeks before the final operation," says Siri, who has followed her gaze. "He turned five just before he died. It was after that I had the idea for Callocain."

Anna nods. It's strange, but it's never crossed her mind that the inventor of Callocain might themselves be grieving. It barely crossed her mind that there were actual people behind it at all, really: to her there was only Danish Pharma, the big corporate monster. And the whole time it's been Siri. Winter's mother, who once had to let the doctors switch off the machine that was breathing for her son.

"I come and sit in here when I miss him too much," Siri says.

Anna nods again. "I tend to fight," she says. "Or get drunk."

After a while, talking gets a little easier. Siri tells her about how Callocain was developed, about all the people who will now be able to get help, and it's obvious how much it means to her. But although Anna listens, her many unanswered questions are still eddying around at the back of her mind, waiting to be asked. She decides to begin with the most important.

"You know what happened this morning, right?" she asks when Siri finishes at last. "Thorsten had an allergic reaction at the university. His heart stopped." She pauses a moment, to lend the words weight. "Funny timing, don't you think?"

Siri looks at her uncomprehendingly. "How do you mean?"

"Well, that it happened right before he was due to speak to Kamilla about Shadi's calculations. Of course, I was the only one who knew about that." Anna holds Siri's gaze. "Except that the two of us were together when Shadi told me, do you remember? It was a few seconds before you made that very important phone call outside."

Siri jerks to her feet. "If you really believe I had anything whatsoever to do with that, then I think you'd better leave."

Her face is utterly open; there's nowhere to hide. You can't look like that if you're lying, can you?

"I get that you're angry I lied to you," Siri says, "and I'm sorry about that. But that—I could never do that."

"No," says Anna. This is Siri after all. Siri, who lay on Anna's bed and spoke so softly that Anna had to hold her breath to hear her; Siri, who can throw her head back and laugh so hard that all the world expands. Even if she hasn't told the whole truth, it's still her. "No, of course you couldn't."

SHADI

SHADI IS STANDING OUTSIDE THE Psychology Department, doing what under normal circumstances Emil would have done for her. She's pulling herself together. Because, obviously, she'd a thousand times rather drop the whole thing and rush home. She has no idea if she'll be able to say what she wants, or what the consequences will be if Kamilla actually listens to her. Thorsten said he would do the meeting alone, to keep Shadi out of it as much as possible, so that must mean coming forward is a risk. But she can't reckon with that now. She straightens her back—she read somewhere that you can trick yourself into believing you're more confident than you really are. If you breathe calmly, make sure your body language is open. Throttle the urge to cut and run.

She thinks again of Thorsten. His wheezing breath, that swollen face as they took him away. She's already let him down once. How can she tell him she let the whole thing fall apart the minute he was out of sight, that she didn't even try? There's no way. And right now, there isn't anybody else. Anna got so weird when she showed her the picture of Anton, and pedalled off almost without saying goodbye. If anybody's going to talk to the boss, it has to be Shadi.

"Excuse me?"

Kamilla, whom Shadi has only seen a few times before, is sitting at the desk in her large corner office with a look of concentration on her face. Without giving any sign she's even heard her, she finishes what she was writing. Only then does she look up.

"Yes?"

"My name is Shadi. I'm doing my dissertation with Thorsten."

"Oh right, yes, I recognize you now," says Kamilla. "It was you who found him this morning, wasn't it?"

"Yeah." Shadi takes another step forward. "I was supposed to have a meeting with him. The plan was for him to talk to you afterwards, to show you something we found. Well, actually, it was me who found it. I've been working on some statistics from your grief project." She stops herself, aware that she's getting into a muddle.

"You what?" Kamilla stands up sharply, making the office chair roll back. "What are you saying?"

"Thorsten asked if I could look at something for him, something that didn't seem quite right," Shadi stammers. "So I did the calculations, and there are some results we thought you should see before you issue the press release. I have them here." She pats her laptop bag.

Kamilla has turned pale, and when she speaks again, Shadi realizes the woman in front of her is furious.

"Shadi was it? I'm sure none of this is your fault, that it's Thorsten who has vastly overstepped his authority. But if I were you, I would run off home right now and delete everything he ever sent you, as well as every single graph you made. Then I'd do us all a favour and forget this ever happened. Involving a student in research in this manner is either professional misconduct or outright illegal, and I don't think you want to be involved in either of those things."

Shadi realizes she's gripping the door frame so hard her fingers are hurting.

Kamilla raises her voice another notch. "Am I right?"

THORSTEN

THORSTEN IS SWIMMING. THE SPACE around him is white and cool, and he's swimming like he hasn't swum since he went on a holiday with his parents to Croatia—when his body glided through the water, and he hid underneath the rented cabin in protest when it came time to go home.

"Thorsten, are you awake?"

The voice forces him to the surface, and there's a jolt when he hits the bed. Through the slits of his eyes, everything is still white.

"Thorsten, are you with us?"

Who is it that keeps talking to him? He feels exposed, lying in this much-too-soft bed while a female figure stands over him, clothed and authoritative, and somewhere in his foggy consciousness he realizes he's in a hospital. A tremor runs beneath his skin.

Someone raises the head of the bed and gives him a glass of juice, and gradually the fog begins to lift. The woman turns out to be a nurse, and she explains that he came in with anaphylactic shock and that, all things considered, he's doing well. It's hard for him to remember. There was the lightness of the bird's body in his hands, the constricted impossibility of his trachea. And Anton, what about him?

"There must have been something in the coffee," he says in a thin voice. "I always eat oatmeal."

The nurse looks at him in confusion, and he explains that he hasn't had anything except his usual breakfast and the coffee Anton gave him.

"What you've been through looks like an intense but entirely normal allergic reaction," says the nurse, refilling his glass. "There's no reason to think anything out of the ordinary happened here."

Thorsten can't really see how she's so sure it was something he ate himself and not something he was tricked into eating. "I'd like to request a toxicological investigation," he says. "Or whatever that sort of thing is called."

The nurse places a soothing hand on his shoulder. "Thorsten…"

"Is it even safe to be here?" he asks, looking around. He's in a four-person room, the beds separated by a sort of curtain, and the door leading to the corridor is ajar. "What's to stop someone from marching in here and poisoning me again?"

"All right, I think you need to try to relax a little." The expression in the nurse's eyes reminds him of Anita, the way she looked when she was coming to the end of her rope with him. "There's nobody out to get you. You're safe here, and everything is going to be just fine."

Then she leaves. From the bed on his left comes a loud snore; somewhere else there's a wail. Every now and then he hears the sound of bustling footsteps in the hallway. He's got to try to stay awake as best he can. His phone is on the trolley cart, and without bothering to figure out what time it is where Andreas is staying, he calls. He just wants to hear Andreas's voice. Although it hasn't fully sunk in yet, he's come close to losing everything. But no one picks up, and the little green dot next to Andreas's Skype icon, the one that means he's there, is gone.

SHADI

FROM TIME TO TIME SHADI gets up and goes over to the window, standing for a minute before she sits back down again. The sense of holding a glass baton that she must not under any circumstances drop is almost electric. Thorsten is in the hospital, Anna isn't picking up when she calls, and if the truth is that she's already dropped the baton in Kamilla's office, then she almost can't bear it.

Thoughts jut to and fro in her mind. One is telling her to let go, to accept that they've done all they can. When Thorsten is up to it, he can decide whether it makes sense to keep fighting, and maybe he'll even manage to persuade Kamilla to get a second opinion from a new statistician. But it certainly won't be easy, especially not now that Kamilla's press release lauding the wonderful results of their project has just landed in newsrooms all across the country.

Another option is to call someone. Get the health authorities or the Danish Medicines Agency involved, let them be the judge of what's warranted here, and whether the launch of Callocain should be postponed until it's clear how it works. But what is she going to say? *I think they've manipulated the results of the big trial just conducted at* AU, *even though the findings they've announced are really fantastic. You've got to do something! Who, me? I'm a dissertation candidate who dabbles a bit with* SPSS *in my spare time, but I'm pretty sure I've got my calculations correct.* She can predict that conversation far too clearly to dare calling anyone at all.

And then there's the final option, the one that leads her into doubt. Of Thorsten's judgment, of her own ability to interpret the data that has somehow ended up in her charge. What if they're wrong? She's got the impression from Anna that Thorsten has a tendency to go charging off rather wildly once he gets a bee in his bonnet, and although he did seem convincing, he might be completely off-base. He's one man out of an entire research group, and none of the others seem to have any problem with the drop in empathy scores or the blue-and-yellow brain scans. Besides, Callocain must be doing something or it wouldn't work. If the pills Shadi takes didn't affect her brain, she might as well throw them in the garbage. Who's to say Callocain is any different—what if what Thorsten calls a side effect is merely a part of its action, something they've already taken into account?

Years ago, when Shadi was trying various formulations in the hunt for something that might help her, she was gripped several times by the fear of losing herself. She asked Emil if he noticed anything different about her, and made him promise to say if she turned into someone else without realizing. He had smiled and asked, wasn't that the whole point of treatment, to create change, but she had felt only an icy horror at the thought of the pills slowly altering the neural pathways in her brain, making her feel or do things she otherwise never would have done. But when she finally found something that worked, when she felt the anxiety release its hold, like a physical unhitching in her body, she knew she would willingly take all the side effects. Fluctuating sleep quality, nausea, low libido—these were negligible in comparison to the feeling of getting herself back. Who is she to judge what other people are willing to sacrifice?

Restless, she does another brief lap around the apartment, ending up back by the windows overlooking the courtyard. If only she knew why there was a decline in empathy. And why in a few cases it was so steep—did it affect people at random or is there a pattern she has overlooked?

Just as the mob of thoughts is growing too insistent, a memory pops into her head. Something Anna said on that very first day at the library, which now slides into place in Shadi's cerebral cortex like a piece in an outlandish puzzle. Moments later she's got SPSS open and her stats book like a life preserver at her side. Perhaps Anna has unwittingly given her the real key to the data set. It must be possible to check, seeing as it's all right here in front of her. It's just a matter of asking the right question.

She runs her finger down the table of contents, and there it is. *Multiple correlation*, that must be what she has to do, and with each line she reads, she's increasingly sure she's on the right track.

Typing with eager fingers, she enters the command and asks the program to test whether mental illness correlates with a linear combination of the grief score and empathy. Whether the vulnerability Anna talked about in the kitchen that day might be what ties it all together. There. Swiftly she double-checks that the right boxes are unticked. Once she's sure it's all correct, she takes a breath like right before a deep dive, and hits Okay.

CHAPTER SIXTEEN

October 2024

ELISABETH

ANNA HAS DRAWN THE CURTAINS and is looking out over the garden, which has grown wild and unruly in recent years.

"This is where your profile picture was taken," she says. "On the terrace. I've often wondered who you were looking at."

Elisabeth nods. She remembers that day. It was during one of those light, floating periods when Winter had responded well to the latest treatment. "It was my friend who took it," she says, "and that one too." She points at the photo on the desk, the only one in the room that includes all three of them. Her, Winter, and Nala.

It's odd to be here with another person. There's been no one else since she started locking the door, and for some reason, now that Anna has arrived, it's as though the air has grown easier to breathe. Something's different anyway, and she examines herself gingerly, the way you feel around a bruise or the kind of inflamed bumps she used to get as a child. Searching for the tenderness she can see in Anna's face when she looks at photographs of Winter.

"I get that you had to find something to do when he died," says Anna, turning. "But you can't live with it, surely, if the pills have side effects? Thorsten says—"

"Thorsten?" Elisabeth breaks in. "A semi-paranoid professor who accuses people of cheating left, right, and centre? Is he really the best person to rely on here? I've been working with Callocain for more than ten years, and trust me, the pills don't do anything that grief doesn't do a hundred times worse."

"Memories that no longer make you feel anything?" Anna's voice is rising. "People who can't engage with other human beings?"

"That's not true," says Elisabeth. "I promise you it's not true."

But she can see from Anna's face that it isn't enough. And when she assures her that she'll check back through everything again, she really means it. It's in her own interest too: unnecessary side effects aren't good news. She just needs a quiet minute to deal with the situation, without it negatively affecting Callocain's launch.

"I'll double-check everything one more time," she says with emphasis. "All our experiments, all the data sets. If there's anything there to find, I'll fix it. But you've got to understand that this is my life's work, and if these kinds of false allegations start circulating, it could destroy everything."

"And how long is that going to take?" asks Anna. "What about all the people who end up taking the pills while you're still double-checking?"

She looks like she has more to say, but Elisabeth raises her hand. "Wait," she says, and hurries out. She needs to convince Anna, at least until the press conference is over. But as she stands there in front of the medicine cabinet, it dawns on her that it's not just about that anymore. She genuinely wants Anna to believe her.

"I know my pills aren't dangerous," she says when she comes back into the room, holding out a blister pack to Anna. "I've tested them myself."

Anna takes the pink tablets, which Elisabeth would be able to recognize among a thousand others. "They're not the same tests as the ones Thorsten's group did," she says dismissively. "You haven't even studied how they affect empathy."

"No." Elisabeth shakes her head. "You're misunderstanding me. What I mean is that I've tested them. Myself."

Anna turns the packet in her hands, as though she's only just noticed all the empty holes. When she looks up at Elisabeth, the whites of her eyes are shining. "What are you saying?"

"That's how I know they aren't harmful," says Elisabeth earnestly. "I know exactly how they work—I've known since the first prototype. Nobody knows Callocain better than I do, and I would never let anyone else take them if I couldn't guarantee they were safe. Give me six months, and I promise you I'll have looked through everything, and if there's even the tiniest bit of truth to what Thorsten is saying, I'll fix it. Six months, max. Can you do that?"

A little later, once Anna has disappeared down the garden path, Elisabeth goes back up to Winter's room. Carefully she taps the papier-mâché rocket, just as she used to do at Winter's bedtime, and watches it begin its slow, twirling course. It's actually a lovely room. Sunny for much of the day. You could easily put an office in here if you wanted.

She leaves the curtains open and shuts the door behind her, but keeps the key in the lock without turning it. Downstairs, she turns the radiators up to get the heat going, takes a throw from the sofa, and wraps it around herself. Anna would have found out who she is soon enough anyway, and she played off the rest of it pretty well. It doesn't seem like Anna has realized the full extent of her deception. Still, her visit was disconcerting. Maybe it has something to do with what she said about memories, just before she left. That a person probably wouldn't notice when they disappeared. Asking how Elisabeth can be so sure she hasn't forgotten something important about Winter. The thought is hard to countenance. After all, there's nothing left of him but what she recalls; without the cupped hands of her memory, it would be as though her little boy never existed.

That's the nature of doubt, she thinks, giving herself a shake. Once it enters in, it contaminates everything. If she's not careful, Anna's accusatory questions will commingle with the memories of squeaking baby mice and the doubts Anton planted when he first called to warn her that something didn't look quite right. And with this comes the familiar dread: that there is something, after all, that she has overlooked. Despite the notebooks and the meticulous records, despite the thousands of hours she has sunk into the project. The terror that the figures she has worked so hard in the past few months to erase aren't hiding an unfortunate side effect of the pills that she can try to correct when she gets the time, but rather that what's beneath them cannot, in fact, be lived with.

This must be where shame is born, she thinks. When, in a moment of clarity, you see yourself through the eyes of another.

ANNA

"WHERE HAVE YOU BEEN? I'VE been calling and calling." It's Shadi's voice.

"I know." Anna turns away from the wind, which is scratching down the line. "I just had to sort out a couple of things."

She needed a good bracing wind after her visit to Siri, so for the past ten minutes she's been standing outside her flat in a vain attempt to organize her thoughts.

"You were right!" says Shadi. "The people who are already psychologically vulnerable are the ones who are hardest hit by grief. But they're also the ones who experience the biggest drop in empathy when they take Callocain. It's like their brains are over-sensitive somehow—everything affects them so badly!"

Shadi's words come thick and fast, so different from their normal, tentative rhythm. She repeats that Anna was right about vulnerability, but in the moment, Anna has no idea what she's talking about.

"They've got to listen to that, don't you think?" Shadi finishes, out of breath.

"Who?" asks Anna, mostly to buy time.

"Thorsten's boss, for one. I didn't even get to show her what we found before she threw me out."

"Okay, well, in that case there's not much more we can do, is there?" says Anna. "I think we should stop now, Shadi, and let other people deal with it if it turns out there are any issues. I mean, how sure are you about this, really?"

How quickly things change. A few days ago Anna would have relished the opportunity to take on the mighty Danish Pharma, and now everything's been turned on its head. Can it really be that banal? If you're deep enough in love, morality falls by the wayside?

"What do you mean?" Shadi sounds confused now. "It won't be long before people are buying these pills at the pharmacy and thinking everything's fine, when in fact some of them are turning into entirely different people. We've got to do something, don't we?"

Anna lets herself tilt forward until her forehead touches the cool concrete wall. If only Shadi had lost courage, the way she'd anticipated, this conversation would have been much easier, but for some reason it seems like the opposite is happening. Again she tilts forward, and this time she presses her head so hard against the wall that the tiny indentations bore into her skin. Then she says it. "I thought you were all about the pills."

She can hear Shadi's intake of breath at the other end.

"What are you talking about?"

"I'm talking about Cipralex for anxiety and OCD, a tablet a day from the packet in the bathroom. What makes Callocain so different from what you're taking yourself?"

"I take that medication because it helps me," says Shadi, giving weight to every word. "I know the side effects I'm risking, and I take the pills anyway because the alternative is much worse. It must be nice to be above that sort of thing, Anna, but have you considered that maybe I know exactly how important this is because I've been there myself?"

Somewhere deep down Anna knows Shadi is right, but it's too late to stop now. Without fully realizing it, she must have made a decision on her way back from Siri's. "I just think it's hypocritical," she says, "and I don't get why this is our fight. Just because Thorsten has run off on one of his wild goose chases, that doesn't mean we have to screw everything up too."

"What is the matter with you?" Shadi asks again. "You were against Callocain from the start. And now that we've found out there actually *is* something wrong with it and we can make a difference, you don't want any part of it?"

Anna winces. She doesn't like talking to Shadi like this or badmouthing Thorsten. If not for him, she'd have dropped out of her studies several times. But Siri promised her there was no issue with Callocain. Would she be taking them herself if there was? She had stood there in Winter's room, looked Anna firmly in the eye, and sworn there was nothing dangerous about the tablets.

"I need to go."

The phone burns against her ear.

"But, Anna." Shadi's voice is on the point of breaking. "I can't do this without you."

"Sorry," Anna says. Then she hangs up.

Blue Notes

SHADI

ALL SHADI HAS TO DO is lay her clothes out for tomorrow, but every time she tries to count up to the right sweater, the process goes awry. Her fingers stop at the grey one with the turtleneck, but that feels wrong, so she starts again. She speaks the numbers out loud in the room like an incantation. If she can get this under control, then it might still all work out: if only she finds the right sweater, maybe she can push the fear back. *One, two, three,* her hands are clammy, but the black cardigan isn't the right one either, nothing is, and instead of trying again she lets her fingers sink into all that softness. She digs out handful after handful of clothes from the wardrobe and tosses them aside until there's nothing left to count.

When she's finished, all the clothes she has painstakingly washed and ironed and arranged in ruler-straight piles are strewn across the floor. The white top Emil likes so much is slung half underneath the bed, and something about the sight makes her desperately sad. She has to get out.

The balcony door sticks, and the wind is icy against her skin. It's the first time she's been outside today, but she still can't catch her breath. All she can think about is Emil. How easy it would be to call him and ask him to come home, if only she could get the image of him and Lucia out of her head. All day she has been looking for distractions, and when Anna finally picked up the phone, she thought she was saved. That they could meet and talk, that Anna would come and fill the apartment like last time, maybe even ask if she could stay over.

The wind is coming in off the sea in salty gusts. What was it Emil said the morning he left? That their relationship had become a prison, that Shadi had locked them both in tight, was that it? She gasps for breath, leaning even further over the railing. Has she herself become the prison she thought was fear? How do you know which is which?

She stays outside until the cold has made her thoughts sluggish and incoherent, and when she comes back in, she's shivering so violently her back is tight. She can't be in the bedroom, where the clothes are waiting. Instead, she lies down on the sofa with the blanket over her and reads old texts from Emil as the warmth slowly returns. *Sweetheart*, he had written one day in June, *it will all be fine, I promise*. Right now she can't even remember what that was about, but it doesn't matter; she reads the words again and again like a mantra. It's nearly twelve o'clock. She is utterly alone.

ANNA

"DID I WAKE YOU?" ANNA asks, at the same moment her dad asks if anything is wrong.

"Sorry I'm so bad at calling," she says, her throat feeling like it's bruised on the inside, "and visiting."

"Is anything the matter?" he asks again, but how can she ever explain it to him?

"Do you remember the grief pills I talked about?" she asks. She's sitting on the windowsill, thoroughly exhausted. Although it's past midnight, she's only just eaten.

"I do, yes. My doctor has suggested I try them, actually. Seems it's time I got my act together."

At first she thinks she's misheard.

"But that's crazy," she says. "Did they do any sort of test?"

"Not a test, exactly. We talked a bit. I mean, I do have to go back to work at some point."

"But you said no, right?" The lost memories Thorsten told them about, Shadi's psychopath test. Siri, who promised to double-check everything if Anna would only give her time. Right now, the thought of that time makes her sick. "You said no to the pills, right, Dad?"

"They're not available yet, as I understand it, but who knows, when they come." He sighs. "I'm not doing very well, Anna."

"No, of course you're not," she says agitatedly, "you miss Mom. But that doesn't mean you're sick!"

"Maybe not. But like I said to the doctor, it's really you I'm most worried about."

"Me? You're the one who has to write a list to put your socks on in the morning," she protests. "I'm doing fine."

Where has this come from? He's been on sick leave for months, and now suddenly she's the one with the problem?

"We don't talk about this stuff very much," he says. "And that's okay, but I just don't want you to be sad and nobody know about it."

She wants to say something about how her way of grieving has got to be at least as good as his, but the words clump together in her mouth. After all, how much understanding has she shown to him? She's spent most of the last month trying to prove that the grief diagnosis is a mistake, and that she herself certainly doesn't fit the criteria. This is the first time she's considered that maybe her father does.

"Will you promise not to take the pills? There must be other options." She hesitates. "Maybe we could look into it together?"

"Maybe we could."

All the things contained in his voice. His vaguely slouched back, the shuffle in his step, blurring with the recollection of a dad who could hold her weight by one arm as she hung from it. The one who could do anything.

"Anyway." He clears his throat. "It's late."

"Yeah." Anna swallows through the ache. "Sleep well, Dad."

"Sleep well, my girl."

THORSTEN

THORSTEN'S FIRST THOUGHT IS THAT he must have taken a blow to the head. Andreas is in Asia, Thorsten is in Skejby. Of course it isn't his voice he can hear.

But there he is. By the bed in a few long strides, bending over Thorsten into a hug. Tall and slim and tanned in shorts and sandals, as though he's just stepped out of another world and forgotten what October means in Denmark. He smells strong and dusty.

"Good morning," he says, smiling, and it really is him. The hospital apparently called Anita, who got hold of Andreas just as he had landed in Beijing, and it was no big deal to hop on a plane to Denmark. "Mum didn't think I should cut my trip short, but I was coming home soon anyway." He smiles again. "You just sped things up a bit."

For the first time since Andreas was small, they're holding hands. Andreas is sitting on the edge of the bed while Thorsten tries to explain what happened.

"I must have eaten something," he concludes, unable to bring himself to tell Andreas about everything else. That will have to wait. "But what about you? What have you been up to since last time?"

It's comforting to have Andreas there, and slowly but surely the wariness loosens its grip. At first, Thorsten is attentive, absorbing everything his son says, but soon his eyes droop shut, and the strangest images accompany the tales of colourful markets and people doing Qigong in the parks. Just before Thorsten falls asleep, he could swear he smells the vegetables sizzling at the roadside kitchens.

He wakes again with a start, mouth dry and head full of cotton wool. Andreas pats his hand and says he's been asleep for more than an hour.

"Someone called Svend dropped by with that." He nods at a bouquet on the bedside table. "He'll come again tomorrow."

Then he goes off to find some food, and Thorsten manages with some difficulty to take out his phone.

Shadi picks up immediately, but she sounds oddly switched off, and it's a struggle to get out what he wants to say.

"Shadi?" he interrupts as she begins once more to apologize for not being able to inject him with the EpiPen.

"Yes?"

"I'm trying to say thank you here. If you'd got there just a few minutes later, I'd have been dead."

She mumbles something he doesn't catch.

"Tell me," he asks, "was I the only person in the office when you got there?"

Shadi confirms that he was alone on the floor when she went in.

"And you didn't see anybody come out?"

"No," she says. "There was just you."

Perhaps his memory is playing tricks on him, then? He was out for a good few minutes, if the doctor is to be believed. Might easily have killed off a few brain cells. Then again, he can see Anton before him so clearly, can replay their entire conversation. It can't be his imagination.

"Did you notice whether there were two coffee cups on the table?" he asks, but Shadi sounds so miserable when she tells him she can't remember that he decides not to probe any further. "But what happened next?" he asks. "You didn't speak with Kamilla, I suppose?"

"I tried," she answers, to his great astonishment, "but it went really badly."

"Did you show her your calculations?"

"She refused to look at them. She said you'd broken the rules by even sharing your data with me, and that I should delete everything straight away if I didn't want to get in trouble. And Anna's out, I don't know what's going on with her, but she isn't on our side anymore."

Is she crying? It sounds like it. Thorsten struggles to sit up—it's amazing how weak you feel after a day in bed.

"Oh, for God's sake," he exclaims. "Hang on a minute."

Using both hands he manages to hoist himself into a position he can tolerate.

"I'm back. You mustn't believe what Kamilla says. You haven't deleted anything, have you?"

"No, but it doesn't matter now. Kamilla's in all the papers this morning, praising Callocain to the skies, and today is the day Danish Pharma gives its press conference too. I'm really sorry, Thorsten. It's too late."

"Nonsense," he says, pushing himself even further upright, although the effort makes his vision go dark. "Of course it's not too late."

By the time they've hung up, the fatigue is bone deep. But he has one more call to make.

"Thorsten Gjeldsted from Aarhus University here," he says when he's put through. "I'm afraid I won't be able to take part in your press conference, but I'd like to put two of my colleagues on the list instead."

ELISABETH

THE TAXI HONKS OUTSIDE. ELISABETH's white dress hangs razor-sharp off the hanger. She's been saving it till last. Now she steps into it, slipping the cool fabric over her hips and zipping up the back. She looks around; it's obvious how empty the house is now that Anna has been there. A good estate agent would probably call it minimalist, but she knows better. This is a waiting room.

The taxi beeps again, and she straightens up. It's time.

"Did you see?"

Marcus shows Elisabeth his phone. It's an article in *Jyllands-Posten* featuring Kamilla, who is explaining that although they still need to thoroughly review the results, it's clear that the grief project will make a substantial contribution to science's understanding not just of Callocain but of the nature of grief itself. She is quoted directly as saying that AU found no cause for concern, and although she goes on to talk about the brain scans and how the memories of the deceased appeared to become less emotionally charged, making them easier to cope with, that aspect is downplayed to such an extent that it will go over most people's heads. The empathy test doesn't get a mention.

As the taxi pulls up outside Danish Pharma, Elisabeth's telephone rings.

"I'll just take this," she says to Marcus, and climbs out. "There's plenty of time, I'll see you in there."

There are numerous cars parked outside the main entrance, so she goes around the back, where she can talk in peace. When she asks Anton why he's calling, the answer is a whimper in her ear.

"Did you hear that Thorsten is still in the hospital? What if they find out it was me?"

"They won't."

"But what should I say if someone asks?"

She sighs irritably. "What is there to say? You were chatting, he collapsed, and you ran for help. Isn't that right?"

"Yes, but I'm sure they can trace that sort of thing, and he knows it was me who brought him the coffee."

"That doesn't prove anything." A car comes puttering around the corner, and Elisabeth retreats further toward the wall. "He could have eaten something with nuts in it, that sort of thing happens all the time. Now pull yourself together, Anton, for the last time. Just go about your business like normal, do your job, and keep a low profile until this has blown over."

She glances at her watch. Ten minutes until the press conference begins.

"It'll all work out, I promise. In an hour's time the worst will be over, and then I will never ask you for anything ever again. Can I count on you?"

There's silence on the line. This is absolutely the last thing she can expect to get out of the geeky statistician, that much is clear. Perhaps she's already pushed him too far. It sounds like he's at a breaking point, and if that happens, none of the dirt she has on him will matter. They both know by now that he's got more than enough to take Elisabeth with him if he goes down. Whether she likes it or not, they're in this together.

"Anton?"

And then, at last, come the words she needs to hear: "You can."

A burst of applause sweeps through the hall as Marcus passes her the microphone.

"Let's hear it for Elisabeth Nordin," he shouts. "The cool brain and beating heart behind the development of Callocain!"

Elisabeth takes the microphone and waits until the din has subsided. "We here at Danish Pharma have spent many years ensuring that we can launch as good a product as possible," she begins, "which is why we welcome the reassuring news that a major research team from Aarhus University has just presented results that both cement Callocain's unique effect on persistent grief and also help us to understand more precisely how Callocain can work as effectively and safely as it does."

"That's not true." A voice from the floor. Elisabeth blinks—it's hard to make out individual faces. It was a woman who shouted, but there's no one Elisabeth immediately recognizes, and when no one comes forward she decides to ignore it. But she gets no further than an intake of breath before the voice pipes up again: "It just looks that way when you hide the side effects."

The crowd is stirring at the edge of the stage. A few journalists step aside, and Elisabeth catches sight of a dark-haired young woman with darting eyes. Can she really be the one who shouted? She looks like she wouldn't hurt a fly, nothing like the usual activists. And how did she get in anyway?

"I'll have to request that we leave all questions until after the presentation," says Elisabeth, staring directly down at the young woman. Then she lets seriousness transform into a big smile. "I have wonderful news to share with you today, actually. It's no secret that we at Danish Pharma love being the first to come up with new drugs, setting the standard for treatment of mental illness, and today it is my great pleasure to inform you that in only a few weeks, Callocain will be accessible to those who need it all around the country. Danish Pharma has—"

"Excuse me?" It's the young woman from before. "Aren't you going to say anything about how Callocain affects memory, and how it makes people stop caring about the loved ones they've lost?"

Her voice keeps cracking. She's petrified, thinks Elisabeth, and something about this realization makes her more relaxed, even as it dawns on her what's happening—who this young woman must be. She approaches the edge of the stage, bends down, and speaks so quietly that only those closest to her can catch it.

"Listen to me, Shadi. You're ruining our press conference. Now—I want you to leave before I call security and have you escorted out, is that understood?"

For a moment, she and the young woman lock eyes, and Shadi looks so timid that Elisabeth feels like laughing out loud. How ridiculous of her to think she could barge in here and change anything.

"This young lady must have got our press conference confused with an open mic night," she says, directing the words toward the hall. She pulls a little face, which thankfully makes a few people laugh. She can feel self-assurance like a tickle down her spine—it's a game she could play in her sleep. Speaking with renewed energy, she begins to talk about the upcoming launch of the world's first grief medication, but at that moment a new voice cuts across hers, coming from the very back of the room.

"Hey, Shadi!"

The noise sends a jolt down Elisabeth's neural pathways. She stares across the crowd, and there she is by the entrance, waving like a madwoman with both hands above her head.

"Keep going, Shadi!" she yells. "Tell them about the psychopath test!"

SHADI

THE ROARING SEA THAT HAD filled Shadi's ears is slowly receding. She can feel her hands again, the placement of her feet on the floor. Anna is here.

Elisabeth has ground to a halt onstage, and a murmur has broken out among the journalists and other guests, standing there with their wineglasses and nuts and baffled stares. If she wants to spit out what she came to say, it's now or never.

"There's something you need to know before you buy this pack of lies about Callocain," she cries into the hall. "I'm a student at Aarhus University, and I've got access to data that shows these pills can have serious side effects!"

There is silence in the large room now, and in front of her a journalist holds up his camera a little hesitantly. She wonders if her parents will hear about this, her sister?

"I take medication every day myself, so I know how important it is that the information on the leaflets is trustworthy. We need to be able to rely on the science, otherwise everything falls apart."

She wrote down reams on her way here, things she was supposed to remember to say. But there isn't time to fish out her notes—she just has to open her mouth and hope the right words come out.

"The research project at AU was sabotaged. Someone, maybe the statistician who processed the data—who, funnily enough, used to be employed here at Danish Pharma—has made it look as though Callocain is harmless. But that is a lie."

A fidget ripples through the front rows, and then Anna is at her side. Her hair looks like she tumbled straight out of bed and onto her bike. She takes Shadi's hand and gives it a squeeze.

"The truth is that Callocain affects our ability to empathize with others," Shadi persists. Her voice is still shaking, but there's nothing to be done about that. "And almost the worst part is that it has the biggest impact on people who are already fragile to begin with. The more vulnerable you are, the better the pills work, and the greater the risk that you will experience a reduction in empathy. You don't even know it's happening—you just feel like your grief is lifting. And who wouldn't want to keep taking a pill that can do that?"

Another squeeze from Anna's hand. She nods in the direction of the main door, where Shadi can see the security guard who let her in half an hour ago. He's heading toward them with a phone pressed to his ear.

Anna turns to the stage, and Shadi follows her eyes. She'd completely forgotten about Elisabeth, but the research leader is standing there still, oddly forlorn, with the microphone dangling from her hand. Her expression is impossible to read, but there's no question it's them she's looking at. And when Anna speaks, it's as though she is addressing only her. "Of course people should get help if they're struggling," she calls out, and the words are like a great song, filling the whole hall. "But Danish Pharma wants us to forget love in order to escape pain. Can we live with that?"

Afterwards, Shadi decides that this was the right place to stop, even though there was plenty she didn't get to say. But as it's happening, as security grabs hold of them, it feels intense. Unyielding fingers seize her arms, and she and Anna are led toward a back exit, away from the throng. As they go, they pass close to the stage. Shadi tries to catch Elisabeth's gaze, but the elegant woman with the big curly hair only has eyes for Anna. Shadi is hauled off, but over her shoulder she sees that Anna has stopped in front of Elisabeth. The security guard tugs, but Elisabeth halts him with a gesture of her hand. It looks as though she's saying something to Anna, but it's impossible to hear above the racket. Shadi has to twist around to look, but as she reaches the exit, she could swear she sees the lead researcher at Danish Pharma bending down to give Anna a kiss.

CHAPTER SEVENTEEN

FEBRUARY 2025

SHADI

"SAME TIME?"

Clutching one side of the thesis each, they hold it out above the tray.

"One, two, three, let go!"

And there it is. *Complex Grief: Existential Condition or Psychological Disorder?* by Shadi Dadras and Anna Jakobsen.

Shadi is feeling less than assured. Anna banged out the final pages yesterday, and Shadi spent all night reading through them, correcting commas and adding missing words.

"It came out so well!" It's the third time Anna has said that.

"It just feels weird that Thorsten isn't here to evaluate it," says Shadi. "I mean, he's the one we wrote it for after all."

Anna is uncorking a bottle of champagne. It surrenders with a pop, and moments later a plastic glass of effervescent bubbles is shoved into Shadi's hand.

"Cheers!" cries Anna, and they clink glasses noiselessly. "Maybe we didn't overthrow the pharmaceutical industry, but at least we're going to pass. I don't think I've ever been so nuanced in my entire life!"

Shadi laughs, and champagne fizzes in her nose. "The only places where you're nuanced are the ones I wrote for you!"

Anna playfully swats Shadi with the special bound edition of their thesis, which they went halves on. "And you're sure you won't come and see Thorsten?"

Shadi shakes her head. "I'm meeting someone."

"Ah, I *thought* you were all dolled up—knew it couldn't be for my benefit," Anna teases.

As they walk out of the department together, it hits Shadi that this might be the last time they pass through these doors. She does a turn to soak it all in. The university park at their feet, waiting to bud, the stubborn ivy on the brickwork, Anna in her mailbox-red down jacket.

"By the way, did you get a response to your appeal?" Shadi asks.

Anna shrugs. "I haven't checked."

"You idiot! So, we don't even know if you're a real psychologist or not."

"I'll do it later," Anna promises. "I'll text you if there's a reply."

She gives Shadi a quick hug, then she's on her bike. Her breath trails behind her like elven mist as she cycles off.

Emil is there already when Shadi arrives. She spots him from way up the road. Why is she so nervous? It's only Emil.

"Hi." He gets up off the bench, standing a little awkwardly with his hands dangling limply at his sides.

He looks skinnier, she thinks. She remembers the feel of his hips against hers, of nestling against his back with one leg over him and her arm around his chest. "Hi."

They step forward at the same time, and for a moment his cheek rests against hers. Then they let go.

It's the first time she's seen him in nearly four months. His nose is red and he's wearing a hat she doesn't recognize. Somehow he feels new, standing there, but of course it's still him. The man who kissed her at the graduation party, when she couldn't quite wrap her head around what was happening, the man she made a home with, who listened to her worries and tugged on countless door handles for her sake.

She can see he's feeling the pressure. A couple of months ago, when she was finally ready to call him, he spent the first ten minutes apologizing, and now he starts again. Before it was like he expected her to be angry, but that isn't how she feels. Not now anyway.

"It's okay." She puts her hand on his arm. "Why don't we walk for a bit?"

It's colder than she'd realized, but still—it's nice to be here with Emil. She asks about his job, what it's like living with his cousin. He says he read her article in *Politiken*.

"I saw that press conference you guys hijacked too," he says. "Some of it's on YouTube. Looked pretty crazy."

"Yeah, it was…" Shadi struggles to find the words. She's watched the clip herself several times, and each time she's as surprised as the last to find it's her doing the shouting.

"What actually happened afterwards?" asks Emil.

"Not much. That lead researcher obviously has friends in high places. Thorsten told me several of the university's other projects are funded by the Danish Pharma Foundation. It's one hundred per cent independent of Danish Pharma, of course—" Shadi draws quotation marks in the air "—but I think an ambitious boss might well be willing to overlook a few things when that kind of money is at stake."

"Is that really how it works? That's nuts." Emil kicks a branch.

"It's also hard to prove there was anything fraudulent going on," Shadi explains. "That stats guy made a few technical decisions that just happened to be quite significant. Removed a couple of the patients, did one sort of test instead of another, stuff like that. So I guess it's just up to the next project to do it better."

As they turn toward the greenhouses, their hands reach for each other seemingly of their own accord.

"I've missed you," she blurts out.

Emil stops abruptly in the middle of the path. "You have?" He's squeezing her hand so hard it hurts. "I'm so sorry," he says again, "and I can't even explain to you why I did it. I think I was turning into a bit of a mess."

She shakes her head. "I think most of what you said that night was probably true. Everything had become so narrow."

He nods. Now it seems almost as though he's the one looking afraid.

"But it's also just the way I am," she says. "I'll never be the kind of person who's out every weekend, and there are really only a few people I want to spend my time with." She can't help laughing at herself. "Is that awful?"

"Nah, not really. But you probably shouldn't go around telling many people apart from me."

That smile. She could still ruin everything.

"We don't need to live together either," she says cautiously. "Maybe we could just..." She pauses.

"See each other?" Emil suggests. There's a droplet hanging from the tip of his nose, and his eyes are bright.

"Exactly," she says, and lifts her face to his as she has done so many times before. Rising up onto her tiptoes, she folds her arms around his neck. "Maybe we could just start with that."

THORSTEN

WHAT THORSTEN MISSES MOST ARE his students. Svend gives a yelp of derisive laughter when he says that, but it's true. The concentrated faces turned toward him during class, the questions they struggle to formulate at the beginning of the year and that are darting off like finely whetted arrows by the end. The pleasure of delving into a subject with someone discovering it for the first time. And although there was something special about Anna, she wasn't the only one who occasionally dropped in for a chat about an intriguing article or a thorny topic. He misses all of that.

"When a failed professor sits musing on the sun," he says, smiling, as Anna walks into the clinic. "Did you submit it?"

"You'd better believe it." She hands him the bound copy of the thesis, which is so handsome they must have had it specially made at a printing house. "Just for you. It's from Shadi too. Have a look at the next page."

He does as she says, flipping past the title page, and there, after a brief foreword, is a dedication to Thorsten, with thanks from Shadi and Anna, and then a couple of handwritten lines with Anna's name and a big, wonky felt-tip heart underneath.

Dear Thorsten, without you this would never have been possible. And by this, of course, I mean me being a psychologist. Thank you.

He reaches out and gives her a hug. "It's been a pleasure."

They sit down in the kitchen. He shares the place with two other psychologists who eat lunch together every day, and so far, it seems to be working. After many years behind a desk, there's something humbling about sitting once again in front of the people it's really all about, talking to them about their troubles in the hope that his words might offer them a new perspective. He'd worried that being fired from AU would make it impossible to get a new job, but in private practice he has entered another world. Here it's his experience that counts, maybe his friendly smile on the website, and it won't be long before he has a reasonable number of clients.

"How are you feeling?" asks Anna, giving him a probing stare. He's noticed it too. At first he thought it was just the kilogram or two he'd lost in the hospital, but it's more than that. The whole episode—being admitted, being fired—has wrought a change in him. Shrunk him somehow. He smiles at her. The thick yellow sweater lends her a soft, almost cozy look that suits her. She appears, thankfully, to be doing well.

"It could be worse," he says. "I could be six feet under, and look, here I am nattering away with my favourite ex-student."

"You're still following, aren't you?"

He doesn't need to ask what she's referring to. Every time they've spoken in the last few months, the grief project and Danish Pharma have come up. He nods. "It's sold to the USA? I saw that, yes."

Anna spits a stone into her palm and takes another date from the bowl. "I don't get it!" she says. "How can they just keep plowing forward? We get on live TV and tell everyone they manipulated the results, and what happens?"

Thorsten can't help laughing at the outraged look on her face. "I know," he says. "But I've spoken to the Danish Medicines Agency, and they promised me they'd keep an extra close watch on Callocain. If they get enough complaints, I think they'll take action."

"But you said it yourself." Anna throws out her arms. "It makes people feel better, so why would they complain? And what are their families supposed to say—*It feels like he loves me less? It's as though she's become a different person?* Good luck pinning the blame on a little pink pill."

Thorsten shakes his head. She's right, of course. He tried to call Mikkel several times after getting back on his feet last autumn, but he never picked up, and Thorsten doesn't know how that situation turned out. He's considered getting in touch with Louise—in fact, he felt like calling all the trial participants and their loved ones after he was fired—but then again. It's not a trivial thing, meddling with people's lives; that much he's learned. You've got to be careful playing God. And what about all the people who are feeling better? How is he supposed to convince someone like Vibeke that she ought to stop the treatment? Doesn't she have a right to decide for herself what she wants to sacrifice? In the end, he let sleeping dogs lie.

"I suppose you'll be looking for a job now, eh?" he asks, patting the finished dissertation.

Anna grimaces. "Not sure I can think of anything I'd like," she says, and for a moment her eyes are quite empty.

"You'll find something," he says. "Maybe it'll look a little different from the rest of us, that's all. You play the blue notes, you know."

Anna frowns. "I do what?"

Thorsten is thinking of the album at home on the record player, of the trumpet's playful flight.

"You play outside of the scale," he explains, "but so did Miles. It's a good thing." He smiles at her and gets to his feet. "But hey— stay in touch, will you?"

"Of course!" She gets up too, slips on her jacket. "We should have one of those PPE groups—isn't that what you call them?— where we sit around and talk about how hard it is to be a psychologist?"

"PPG."

"Exactly. I'll ask Shadi if she wants to join too. She's crossed into enemy lines, did you hear?"

Thorsten looks at her quizzically. He hasn't spoken to Shadi since the day after the press conference.

"Psychiatry," Anna explains. "She's already landed her first job, the little go-getter." She nudges the door open with her hip, raising her hand in farewell. "Look after yourself, okay?"

Then she's gone.

Back in his office, Thorsten sinks into his armchair with a sigh. Most of his things from the institute he's brought with him, but the view is different. Here there are no chattering youths, no green lawns where you can let your mind drift, only privet hedges and asphalt. And the obvious irony that the clinic is situated in a dead end, of all places.

He looks up at the picture of Andreas, which has replaced Hudson on the nail. In it he'd just turned six, if Thorsten remembers correctly; it was taken the summer before he and Anita moved.

"Just the two of us again, then," he says. And sets about preparing for his next client.

ANNA

"YOU'RE SHARP TODAY, ANNA! GOOD energy."

Isam claps her on the shoulder, and he's right—she feels good. Her body is working as it should.

"Thanks," she puffs, blowing an air kiss in Maiken's direction. "I hope that jaw isn't getting too sore!"

Her bike has a flat tire, so she has to take the bus. Along the route she gazes out the window, at scenery she's driven through so many times on her way back from school. Past the stop where she once got off by mistake and ended up having to walk the last few kilometres, sobbing with fury at the side of the road. The new build, where there used to be fields. When she gets off, it's pelting down with rain. For a few seconds she stands there with her face upturned, letting the droplets drum against her skin, then she dashes over toward the main door.

"Ah, here you are," says her dad, smiling.

His dinner menu is horrifying. Frozen meatballs with horseradish and rye bread.

"And veggies," he says, pointing at the jar of pickles. She shakes her head and goes to fetch her mom's bike from the basement. She comes back with cabbage, chickpeas, and a bag full of ingredients for a salad, which she makes while he fries the meatballs, and they switch on the radio like the old days on vacation, singing along with everything that comes on.

Her father's voice rumbles along to "Like a Rolling Stone," in the crazy bass that usually only appears when he's really angry.

In the middle of dinner, he raises his glass. "Well, congratulations on submitting the dissertation," he says. "I never doubted you."

"Oh, stop it." She swats at him. "It's not easy, actually, to make it through a program like that—which you would know if you'd ever set foot in an institute of higher education."

Later, her phone lights up. From time to time, she still catches herself hoping it will be Siri's name that appears. This time it's Shadi's.

Want to drop by the harbour one of these days? We'll celebrate!

"Ha!" she exclaims.

"What is it?"

"Nothing," she answers lightly, "just another poor soul who's fallen for my irresistible charms."

"Goodness."

Her dad undoes his belt and goes into the living room. She hears him sigh as he sits down, then the sound of the TV being switched on. The moving boxes are still over by the cupboard, half-full—they'll have to get that sorted out one day. But for now, she contents herself with sending Shadi a V for victory, then goes in to watch the news beside her dad.

ELISABETH

ELISABETH CAN'T QUITE WORK OUT what to call her state of mind right now. On the surface, not much has happened lately. Marcus has called a few times. Full of strained joviality at first— probably he was hoping she'd tell him it was all a pack of lies. That she didn't know anything, that there couldn't conceivably be any side effects to Callocain, that she had no connection to Anton or his questionable data. And she admitted to nothing. But she protested too little.

Later, Marcus told her the American deal was hanging by a thread, and that the Danish Medicines Agency was calling things into question—showing its teeth. Already, perhaps, it was beginning to dawn on them both that Elisabeth was no longer really present. That she was on something more than temporary leave. And when at last he began to raise the idea that they might be forced to cease production of Callocain, or that the name itself had such negative associations that they'd have to start from scratch with a thorough rebranding, she couldn't even be bothered to reply. She didn't care. Maybe it was her unaccustomed passivity that so enraged him—he screamed into the phone, yelling that she was suspended, that she'd better give the whole situation a wide berth until they had a proper handle on things. That was when she told him she didn't want to be involved anyway. She resigned. And she hung up in the middle of the avalanche of words, which had so immensely little to do with her.

Now here she is, sitting on the terrace in one of the two wooden chairs that should have been put away in the shed for winter, drinking whisky that's been gathering dust on the shelf for years. It's a clear day, almost transparent, but with a blanket over her legs she isn't cold. By her side is a new notebook. Occasionally she reaches for it, and in handwriting that lists steeply to the right she jots down research ideas, fragments of daydreams and little flashes of memory, not knowing what she's going to do with them.

It feels like tidying up, in a room she hasn't entered for a long time. Winter's in there too.

She refills her glass. Really, she supposes, what happens next is up to Anton. At first glance everything points to him, assuming anybody takes the time to properly look. As they commented in the paper a few weeks after the fateful press conference, Anton is well-known as a prominent expert in his field; he knows what he's doing. So, why? Why, in this specific trial, would all that go out the window? He doesn't obviously benefit from making Callocain look good, unless, as Thorsten was quoted as saying, someone—from his former workplace, perhaps—had dirt on him, or was paying him a lot of money. Elisabeth had surprised herself by laughing out loud in her front room and remarking that, in this particular case, it was a matter not of either-or but both-and. Personally, she found it rather amusing.

As she sees it, Anton might easily crack—if somebody knows to keep the pressure up. It's always been his greatest fault, his weakness of character. The terrible drop of his hands. And, of course, he will give her up if he himself is caught. But as she sets about tidying the spaces of her mind, opening windows, and letting in fresh air, one thing becomes increasingly clear: none of that really matters. Either way, she has to find a new place to start. And right now, here in the chair on the terrace, it's birdsong that stands out the strongest. A robin, she thinks, busy telling his fellows that this territory is claimed. Images of her little boy and his shadow, running together across the grass.

NOTES

AS THE TITLE PAGES SUGGESTS, this is a novel, not non-fiction, but I'd like to reiterate that here. As I write this, grief is indeed being established as a diagnosis in Denmark, although it's still unclear whether it will be termed prolonged or persistent grief disorder. As yet, however, neither Danish Pharma nor Callocain exist, except in my imagination. And although much of the scientific material in the book holds water, I have sprinkled gaps and little white lies across its pages.

Callocain, by the way, is a play on *Kallocain*, a dystopian science-fiction novel by Karin Boye. The book is about a totalitarian society governed using a truth drug called Kallocain.

ACKNOWLEDGEMENTS

THANK YOU TO MY FANTASTIC agents at the Grand Agency, who make everything happen, and a special thanks to Peter Stjernström for providing the inspiration for Callocain. Thank you to Lise Villadsen, my striped tiger, for reading through the manuscript a thousand times and giving me crucial encouragement along the way. To Heidi Korsgaard for another miraculous save and to my lovely editor Iben Konradi Brodersen for embracing my story mid-process and guiding it home.

I'd also like to thank everyone who helped me by providing valuable information along the way. There are more of you than I have space for here, but without Professor Jesper Mogensen (whose brilliant teaching many of us who studied psychology at Copenhagen University remember) and Professor Morten Grunnet from Lundbeck, who was incredibly generous with both his time and his knowledge, this book would have been much the poorer. Then there is Nete Tofte, who told me about EpiPens, comas, and anaphylactic shock; Marie Kofod Svensson, who led me to Winter's heart disease; Klemens Kappel, who was my inside line on both rigged research and blackmail; Sune Bo, who was my light in the darkness of research at the first tender beginnings of this book; and of course Diana Juncher and Rasmus Hedegaard, who helped me to figure out the grief graphs. Thank you! Also to my workplace, CKB, for once again allowing me leave to write, and to all the good people in Aarhus who opened their homes and their hearts to me when I came on research trips. And, of course, to my long-suffering parents, who let a sullen thirty-seven-year-old teenager move back home to write during the pandemic, when I suddenly found myself without a place to live. And, finally, there are the wonderful readers who pored over my unfinished sentences, trying to make them make sense. Huge thanks to my beta-readers, Rikke Dahl, Sarah Reffstrup Jørgensen, Maria Junggren, and Anne Bach—your thoughts were worth their weight in gold! And, last but not least, my beloved Frederik, whose reading made me, as usual, more frustrated than happy, but who—in part because of that—was once again a huge help. Thank you for all our conversations about life's blue notes.

Diana Juncber

ABOUT THE AUTHOR

ANNE CATHRINE BOMANN lives in Copenhagen, dividing her time between writing and working as a psychologist. She also played table tennis for Denmark and won the national championship twelve times. She is the author of two poetry collections and the debut novel *Agatha*, which became a word-of-mouth success following publication in Denmark and has now been translated into twenty-three languages.

Caroline Waight

ABOUT THE TRANSLATOR

CAROLINE WAIGHT is an award-winning literary translator working from Danish, German, and Norwegian. She has translated a wide range of fiction and non-fiction, with recent publications including *The Lobster's Shell* by Caroline Albertine Minor (2022), *Agatha* by Anne Cathrine Bomann (2021), *Island* by Siri Ranva Hjelm Jacobsen (2021), and *The Chief Witness* by Sayragul Sauytbay and Alexandra Cavelius (2021). She grew up travelling around the world, living in eight different countries. Having first studied music at Cambridge, Oxford, and Cornell, she worked in publishing before transitioning into full-time literary translation. She now lives and works near London.

Colophon

Manufactured as the first English edition of
Blue Notes
in the spring of 2024

Copy-edited by Kaiya Smith Blackburn

Proofread by Stuart Ross

Type + design by Michel Vrana

Printed in Canada

bookhugpress.ca